Jenny Green's KILLER
Junior Year

More KILLER reads from Simon Pulse

Revealers
Amanda Marrone

The Center of the Universe:
Yep, That Would Be Me
Anita Liberty

Crimes of the Sarahs
Kristen Tracy

The Private series
Kate Brian

SIMON PULSE
An imprint of Simon & Schuster Children's Publishing Division
1230 Avenue of the Americas, New York, NY 10020
Copyright © 2008 by Amy Belasen and Jacob Osborn
All rights reserved, including the right of reproduction
in whole or in part in any form.
SIMON PULSE and colophon are registered
trademarks of Simon & Schuster, Inc.
Designed by Mike Rosamilia
The text of this book was set in Adobe Garamond.
Manufactured in the United States of America
First Simon Pulse edition September 2008
2 4 6 8 10 9 7 5 3 1
Library of Congress Control Number 2007943364
ISBN-13: 978-1-4169-6792-7
ISBN-10: 1-4169-6792-3

Jenny Green's KILLER Junior Year

AMY BELASEN & JACOB OSBORN

Simon Pulse
New York London Toronto Sydney

To Abby, Amanda, and Anat,
and to Laura Marsolais
Inspire, create, and do what you love
—A. B.

To Paul Raker, aka "Rake-a-Roni,
the Princeton Junction Treat"
—J. O.

Acknowledgments

Thanks to my exceptionally talented coauthor, Jacob Osborn; to my lit agent, Alex Glass, for being so damn cool and "getting it"; to my editor, Michael del Rosario; to Chris Day and Yuli Masinovsky at UTA for giving Jenny Green her first taste of showbiz; to Mary D'Amico and the RPI Young Actors Guild for helping me discover what I love; to my ex-boyfriends for the starting place of these pages; to Montreal—the most beautiful city on earth; to my mom for the love and grammar corrections; to my father, Alan Belasen (okay, Dad, PhD!) for writing the first book in the family and starting from scratch in America; to Camp Greenberg, my second home; to my siblings—Ari (". . . PhD!"), Anat, Amanda, and Abby—for keeping things interesting; and to my best friends forever, Shelley, Nicole, Jillian, Lolo, and Laura. And special thanks to Ossie Beck for all the love, inspiration, holidays, and fro-yo.

—Amy Belasen

Special thanks to Jason Director, Alex Glass, and Michael del Rosario for the terrific feedback and enthusiasm, and to Michael Simon, Yuli Masinovsky, and Chris Day for the interest and support. And an extra-special thank-you to Amy Belasen, for being such an amazing coauthor and for having so many disastrous relationships. Thanks!

—Jacob Osborn

Jenny Green's KILLER Junior Year

PART ONE

Fall Comes Early
(and So Does Josh Beck)

Chapter ONE

F YOU, LONG ISLAND!

'Twas the end of a long and bitter sophomore year. 'Twas. I just really wanted to use that word. I promise I won't use it again; this ain't Dickens. Seriously, though, sophomore year totally sucked. I broke my toe and couldn't be in the school production of *Grease*, Doug Lapidus took a picture of a huge zit on my nose and broadcast it on Facebook, and that bitch Veronica Cohen stole my prom date Mark Leibowitz.

It wasn't fair! Mark asked me to prom first. You can't change your mind about that kind of thing, not unless you're willing to pay for therapy years down the road when I'm dealing with a major onset of insecurity. And don't tell me I had two more years—there was only one Mark Leibowitz, and he was graduating. I had a huge crush on him and that's how he left me: crushed.

And it wasn't like Veronica was older or anything; she was a sophomore too (a sophomore who was willing to go all the way, but a sophomore nevertheless). She was *supposed* to be one of my best friends.

To make matters worse, Doug Lapidus posted a blog on his MySpace page making fun of me and how I got ditched. And just when my classmates were finally over the whole Facebook weather report, "100 percent Green with a chance of acne on both nostrils," his new blog was posted. What did he have against me anyway? 'Twas a bitter year indeed (last time, I swear).

The annual yearbook signing was a pretty big deal, and all four grades gathered on the football field. Mark Leibowitz, the jerk who ditched me before prom, tactfully ignored me, and I tactfully ignored Veronica Cohen.

Oh, here's one yearbook message worth sharing.

From Richard Titleman: *Jenny, I'll never forget you and the night we had kissing over the LIE.*

Awww . . . It made me forget all about Mark, sort of. Guys. I just love guys. And no matter how many I date or kiss or flirt with, there never seem to be enough. Great, now I sound like a slut. I just wasn't the best at keeping a steady boyfriend.

Okay, so other than Richard Titleman's message, the yearbook signing was just a reminder of how crappy the year had been. I could have sworn I had a million friends at one point, but now it seemed no one wanted anything to do with me: the PPC (Persian Power Crew), the BLT (Boys Lacrosse Team), the ATBOC (All That and a Bag of Chips)—they all huddled in their respective corners and merely snickered when I passed, my yearbook clutched tightly to my chest. Even my own clique, the JAPs (Jewish American Princesses, if you couldn't guess), seemed reluctant to sign. What was I, a leper or something?

It was right there on the football field that I made my resolve: I was getting the heck out of Long Island. There were other seas with cooler fish, and I was confident that outside my little bubble was a big world with lots of guys who would be way cuter than Mark Leibowitz.

I'll admit something now: I was always on the lookout for Prince Charming. He'd sweep me off my feet and take me away in his valiant horsepowered navy blue BMW to the local synagogue, where we'd get married. An expensive reception would follow at the Four Seasons. The full bar would serve Grey Goose whatevers and my Uncle Murray would do his magic tricks and there'd be nondairy fire-roasted veggie salad with grilled chicken and I'd wear a long white Vera Wang gown before which every other girl kneeled and . . . all right, I'm getting a little carried away.

Needless to say, "the one" always lingered in the back of my mind, but it didn't bother me *too* much that I hadn't found him yet. Still, none of my experiences in high school could have prepared me for the utter lameness of the guys I'd soon meet in boarding school. I repeat, and seriously, feel free to scribble this somewhere while you're reading: *None of my experiences in high school could have prepared me for the utter lameness of the guys I'd soon meet in boarding school.* Pretty please, keep this in mind before you blame me for *everything* that happens in the next however many pages.

A little more about myself. How about my name? Jennifer Green. Kind of rolls off the tongue, right? Okay, it's a little corny, so you can just call me Jenny. Anyway, like all good JAPs I was born and raised in Long Island to an overprotective mother with an irritating accent and a workaholic father with terrible sinuses. I was the first of three children, the other two being twins, Abby and Amanda.

My mom smothered me with clothes, my father with jewelry. I love both of my parents and, for the record, don't hold them responsible for my actions in any way. I love you, Mom! I love you, Daddy! Leaving them would be the hardest part.

But it wouldn't stop me; I was determined to wash my hands clean of Long Island. Even if my reputation *hadn't* been destroyed by some dweeb on Cheetos, there was no good reason to go back. I just couldn't deal with my jappy friends always talking about last night's episode of *The Hills* or some deal they'd gotten on Juicy at Bloomingdale's. Can you blame me?

It made me sick just thinking about it. Boarding school seemed like the only logical choice.

"Boarding school?" Mom exclaimed. "What are you, nuts?"

Convincing the folks wasn't going to be easy. There was a lot of crying that night, and pacing, and slamming of doors. Eventually, though, there was the opening of doors, as in Daddy opening my door and saying that if boarding school was truly where I felt I belonged, then it was open for discussion. I had the Green light. Get it?

Next came the long review of which boarding schools were best and why. Daddy said Manhattan had some of the best schools in the country, and it was right next door. But I didn't want Manhattan. In fact, I didn't want a school anywhere in America. America sucked. It was so in-your-face it made me wanna vomit.

The truth was, I'd been scoping out the right school for quite some time. So I let my parents talk until they were so tired that their guards were down, and then I dropped it on them: "Molson Academy in Montreal."

Yes, Molson, as in the beer, had its own boarding school in Montreal, and that was where I wanted to go. They didn't have a dress code, it was only grades 9–12, there was an on-campus restaurant and a TCBY (which is in fact The Country's Best Yogurt) in the cafeteria, and it was far, far away. PS, even though I'm lactose intolerant, TCBY never upsets my stomach. I know, it's like magic or something.

"Montreal? Be serious, Jenny."

"I *am* serious, Mom."

She wasn't having it. "Jenny, our country is fighting a war. There's danger outside the door."

"Exactly, so where safer to be than Canada?"

"It's out of the question. The school's owned by a beer company! Alan, tell her it's out of the question."

"Now hold on," said Daddy. He was on the Internet, looking it up. I knew the credentials would impress him. They had a 98 percent graduation rate, for crying out loud.

Mom was still fussing. "Alan, it's in Canada!"

"Jenny's right, Susie. Canada's safer than the States."

"There won't be any Jews," Mom warned.

Why did I need to be around Jews? Besides, she was wrong, there'd be one Jew. His name was Josh Beck, and he was the secret reason I wanted to go. He was the biggest crush I'd ever had.

It was eighth grade. We didn't talk much and he had a girl-friend at the time, but I'd been eyeing him all year. Then at the Spring Fling we slow-danced to a Gwen Stefani song. He said he really liked me, and my heart melted. Alas, that summer his family moved to Montreal, and he ended up at Molson. I was devastated. If there was one man for me, it was Josh Beck. I was sure of it.

Around midnight Mom caved. If it was what I really wanted, then maybe Molson was the place for me.

It was what I wanted. I wanted to move on to the next destination, to the next phase of my life, to Canada.

Chapter *TWO*

FIRST IMPRESSIONS

It was Mom who wouldn't let me stay in those crappy freshman dorms. Let me explain. Since I applied so late in the year, there were like a zillion complications we had to work through. I felt pretty bad having Daddy jump through hoops, but I'd make it up to him.

First, the school was booked, and the admission deadline was this past January. Daddy fixed that with a few phone calls and a negotiated late admission fee. To ease his pains, I cheated on my entrance exam and landed myself in AP Calculus. We'll get to that later.

The next problem was housing. Because the school was basically filled, the only available housing was in the freshman dorms. They weren't exactly to my liking, but my parents had done so much by that point that I kept my mouth shut. Luckily, Mom felt the same way I did.

"Alan, you're not letting Jenny stay here, are you? Look at the walls—I'm collecting dust just by touching them. And it's so cramped. Where's she gonna keep her dresser?" Then came the loud honking from outside—my sisters waiting in the car. This was late August.

Since Mom had gotten things started, I figured I might as well take a side. "Yeah, it's pretty squishy in here. I don't have any room to study, either."

"All right, all right!" I love my daddy.

So it was back to the housing department, where, after more negotiating, something turned up. All the junior housing was occupied except for one bed in the Female Artists' Colony. The Female Artists' Colony was just a fancy name for a large brownstone house where all the female students with art grants stayed. You know, musicians, painters, etc. It sounded fun!

Bags in hand, we arrived at the front door. "Careful, Alan, that's a Louie!" Okay, so my luggage bordered on jappy, and my mom was super protective of it.

Well, maybe *one* piece wasn't so "precious." Daddy hauled in the duffel bag. Let me tell you about this duffel bag. It was the biggest duffel bag in the world. In all honesty, I kind of hated it, because it was a pain in the butt to lug around and always bumping into things, and that's not to mention how outdated it was, stylistically speaking. The stupid bag must've been at least six feet long, and it was where I stuffed all my lower-tier clothes, blankets, and extra accessories. One day I planned on ditching the thing and upgrading to one of those *really* big suitcases.

Entering, I took a nice look around. To the right was the spacious den with the couches and television. The hallways were long and nonclaustrophobic. The newly redone hardwood floors were sleek and sophisticated. It was a dream. And did I hear footsteps? Who was coming to greet me? A new friend?

Oh wait, those weren't footsteps, those sounded like . . . paw steps. Suddenly appearing in the hall was our inductor into the brownstone: a big, disgusting dog. I think it was a golden retriever.

He was advancing, his wet tongue bouncing in the air, his golden brown fur spotted with dirt. I could already picture the big smelly thing jumping on me or humping my leg, so I quickly bent down to guard my jeans.

"Sit, dog, sit!" I yelled. He was close now. My precious Paper Denims were history!

"Orion!" someone hollered from down the hall. The dog froze in his tracks, just inches away.

Turning a corner was a girl who seemed pretty enough, although she looked kind of old, like in her twenties or something. She had jet-black hair and a hooked nose that somehow suited her. She wore a sleeveless dress, which if you asked me was a big mistake, because as soon as she lifted her arms I saw the most wretched thing in my life—hair. There was a full bush of black hair under her arms, like she was raised by wolves in the Amazon jungle. Didn't she get the memo? It was the twenty-first century now.

"Hi, I'm Raven. I'm the housemother," she said, extending a hand (of course her right one, 'cause *everyone's* a righty—naturally, I'm a lefty). Did she say Raven?

Keeping my distance, I inspected her hands. Her fingernails had dirt under them, and she'd probably never even heard of a manicure. She was like a total hippie. Where had I landed? Was it too late to go back to the dorms? Daddy would kill me.

Then another girl came down the stairs and waved as she headed into the kitchen. Her head was shaved and streaked in rainbow colors, and she was eating like one of those Mediterranean salads that come with your hummus plate that you just kind of pick at and never finish. She definitely looked like a weirdo. Following her was another hippie, who was followed by another weirdo.

The catch of such nice living was thus brought to my attention: The entire house was filled with hippies and weirdos. And when I say filled I mean, like, eighteen other girls. I'd soon discover there was only one non-hippie/weirdo besides myself (that would be Chloe, the coolest girl in the world).

But I had more immediate problems, because Raven's crusty hand was still in the air. Okay, Jenny, I thought, here's your first challenge, making good with the tree people. Daddy shook, but I saw the hesitation. Mom, Abby, and Amanda kind of hid like scared bunnies behind Daddy, where they'd wait until the strange girl with the dirty palms was gone. It was pretty rude, I know, but thankfully they didn't have to live here. I did. I held my breath so as not to take in any fumes. Cautiously I brought forth my hand . . . we shook.

"Nice to meet you," I muttered. We both grinned awkwardly. There, that wasn't so hard. Now where was the nearest sink?

Woof! Woof! "This is my dog, Orion, he's the housedog!" Raven informed us enthusiastically.

Orion wanted attention. Did he have to smell like that? It didn't make things any easier. But I kept reminding myself how important first impressions were, so with my lips quivering, I gave him a timid pat on the back. He liked it. Then he barked right when my hand was near his face, and I jumped back, like, ten feet.

So there would be some adjusting—some major adjusting. Again, that's what going to a new school was about, and I didn't sweat it. It was part of my eye-opening experience, right?

Well, whatever. Let me tell you a little about the campus, because it was killer. It was in its own little corner of the city and basically cut off from civilization by a huge stone wall. Think college. Lots of trees and open areas. Lots of houses on different rows. Kids playing Frisbee, open windows with music blaring, all that good stuff.

Montreal was pretty amazing too—so pretty and clean compared to New York. I couldn't wait to see what adventures it held in store for me. Restaurants, parks, shopping, so much shopping. There was even this street, St. Laurent, that was just littered with bars and good-looking people. Did you know the drinking age is only eighteen in Montreal? I needed to get a fake ID pronto. This was so amazing!

After moving in, we upgraded my phone plan to include Canada, then had an expensive steak dinner at Moishes with the fam. A few days later they were gone. It was sad to see them all go, but exciting, too. For the first time I was on my own, with so many new people!

Chapter THREE

PUTTING THE "HIP" BACK IN "HIPPIE"

Hanging my super-awesome mirror on the closet door, I put the finishing touches on my room. I caught a glimpse of myself. My hair was shoulder-length and brown. My brown eyes had a touch of hazel to them (or maybe that was just my contacts), and if you looked closely enough you'd spot light freckles on my smooth face. I was totally cute.

"Jenny, you're not one of those materialist Long Island chicks, are you? I mean, look at all these clothes!"

Ugh. Way to kill the moment. That was Jacinda, my roommate. She had a bong in one hand and some philosophy book in the other (her "leisure" reading). Her special art was spoken-word poetry. She was camped out in the corner of our room on a futon that reminded me of Joseph's Amazing Technicolor Dreamcoat.

Although she was my roommate, we hadn't really talked like, you know, the way friends talk. Almost every night she'd slept at the Male Artists' Colony, where her hairy boyfriend lived, and whenever she *was* around we just kind of ignored each other. What saddened me was that beneath her freaky braids that had never been brushed and her backless hippie shirt showing off bacne in three phases (sores, scars, and unpopped pimples) was a very pretty girl crying to get out.

"What can I say? I have a weakness for designer clothes." I tried to play it cool.

"It's totally warped. You should donate half of your wardrobe to Village des Valeurs or something. Have you read this book? It's about Buddhism. You need to enlighten your mind. Tabernac, Jenny! You've got your own computer and television and everything."

And then it came, her "talent": "The material world is but a material pearl of false material wis*dom*, notice I say dumb because material numb, is in all of us, there will be a bus, there will be a bus, let's dispense the ignorance."

Ummm . . . yeah. PS, for those of you who noticed the word *tabernac* and thought, what the heck is tabernac, it's like this old-school Quebecois curse word. Don't worry, it threw me off at first too.

I was still adjusting to Canada and hippies and intrusive poetry and dealing with a lot of language barrier issues. There was like five times more French than English, and I almost got run over crossing the street because instead of DON'T WALK there was some word I couldn't even pronounce.

I could've definitely used someone to break me in, someone

named Josh Beck, perhaps. But guess what? I asked around, and he lived in Montreal with his parents, meaning he wouldn't be around until classes started. Those late August days at school weren't exactly the greatest. And classes hadn't even started yet.

Anyway, having said her piece, Jacinda lit the bong and sucked up the heavy smoke. The water gurgled, and soon after a thick gray cloud erupted from her mouth. Hoarse coughing followed. "One day we'll show you the light, eh?"

If that was "the light" I'd take mucus-free lungs, thanks. I went back to looking at myself in the mirror and deciding whether my shirt was too big, trying to ignore the Dalai Lama's stoner cousin as best I could.

But the smoke soon clustered around me and forced a cough from my precious lungs. It hurt! I hoped I wasn't gonna get stoned; I just knew I'd get completely paranoid or something. And through the haze I swear Jacinda was grinning ear to ear. She was happy to see me in pain. I said nothing, because I didn't want to get things off to a bad start. I was burning inside.

"Do you mind?" I asked kinda politely.

"Hey, this is my room too, Jenny. Just learn to relax and we'll get along fine."

"But it's *my* room too. We both have to live here, and that means compromise. Everything can't just go your way."

"*My* way!"

"Jacinda, the rug needs to go."

"What are you talking about?"

"The floors are gorgeous here. Don't you realize they were just redone?"

"Uh, yeah. I've been living here for two years."

"Well, look at this rug. It's a cheap Mexican print that looks like it was found on the street."

"I like this rug."

"But what the F, Jacinda? I mean, I have to deal with the smoke, the random crumbs you leave lying around, the empty glass bottles you cover with wax, the shirts you leave hanging on every chair. Please, the only thing I ask is we lose the rug."

"No way! My old boyfriend got me this rug."

"If he's an old boyfriend, why do you want to be reminded of him? It's the only thing I ask!"

It killed me. Here we were in this amazing house at this amazing school and Jacinda insisted on living like a slob. She kept all her underwear, shorts, and socks in one drawer. One drawer! If you could even call it a drawer. It was more like a gigantic Tupperware container. Compared to my dark espresso oak dresser and amazing full-size bed with memory foam pillows and hypoallergenic comforter, Jacinda's stuff looked like it was bought from a homeless person's shopping-cart clearance sale.

Her only luxury was the crusty hot plate she kept by the window. Thanks for cooking in the room, Jacinda, I was so glad to be sharing my living space with you and the entire insect kingdom. Seriously, she was a total slob.

But I had her thinking about the rug, which was a start.

"Jacinda," I said nicely, "I love the futon"—that was a big lie—"and I love the big sheet you have hanging on the wall"—that was an even bigger lie—"but please, this rug looks like it came with the house when it was built at the turn of the last century. It's gross, Jacinda." That was not a lie. "It must go."

Jacinda took another big hit from the bong. *Keep going*, I thought, *get nice and stupid and maybe your better judgment will kick in.* I gripped my stuffed bear and lifelong companion, Herman. Herman ruled.

Jacinda finally caved. "All right, Green, the rug can go. But if we're gonna get along, you need to chill the fuck out, deal?"

"Deal." And as more dirty pot smoke filled the room, I grabbed the rug and made for the door.

In the hall I saw an ashtray and emptied it into a garbage bag, then threw the bag out with Jacinda's crappy rug. I was on a mission now, so while I was at it, I cleaned the bathroom using these dirty handkerchiefs that were slung over the edge of the tub. Who uses handkerchiefs to clean, anyway? Hadn't they heard of Windex and paper towels? Or mops? Or better yet, cleaning ladies? I threw the soggy handkerchiefs away as well.

Then later that night a hippie named Sasha and a weirdo named Amber had a long conversation with me. Apparently the ashtray was still in use, since it had "roaches" in it.

"Roaches are bad," I told them.

Sasha replied, "Not the insects, Jenny. And even the insects aren't bad. They're animals, just like you and me."

"So are poisonous snakes, but I don't want them in the house either."

Amber held up one of the used handkerchiefs that had somehow escaped. "And what aboot these, Jenny?" Amber was from Manitoba, so her accent was Canadian, not French Canadian. I usually laughed when she spoke for those first two weeks. "Why are you laughing?"

"It's nothing, Amber."

She waved the dirty handkerchief in the air. "I'm soory, but you see these, Jenny? These are mine. I wear them."

I didn't even know how to respond to that one. It was like the house had been cut off from time. Maybe it was a government experiment or something. I mean those rags were like developing rust. I couldn't believe they put them in their hair. I needed to get these girls some butterfly clips.

This was life at Molson for the first two weeks. It seemed that every corner I turned there was an unshaven armpit or a half-smoked joint. When the hallways didn't smell like paint, they smelled like dirty bong water. Amber had a tattoo of the morning on her chest, Sasha a lip ring. I wasn't sure how these things came to symbolize the free spirit (or the morning), but they spoke novels about these people. One night I heard two of the hippies in the den saying how not wearing shoes brought you closer to nature. Closer to dirty feet was more like it, and closer to dirty hardwood floors.

And there were always these random guys strolling through the halls like cavemen. Sometimes they were naked as apes, their used condoms and plastic beer cups littering the floor behind them once feeding time had ended. I'd barely even *seen* a naked man before moving in.

Feeding time was grossly frequent, by the way. At any given hour you could hear an "artist" in the throes of passion, screaming loud enough to drown out some other girl playing the violin or the bongos and singing Lilith Fair or whatever it was. For a virgin (yes, I was still a virgin at the time), it was terrifying.

Should I leave? I kept asking myself. I mean, I was an outsider in a house where the normal outsiders were now insiders. But where would I go?

It was meeting Chloe that saved me. There were so many girls that it took a few days before Chloe and I found each other. I was cleaning weirdo hair out of the sink when I heard the voice behind me. "Gross."

"What's more gross is that it's not mine."

"Ewwwww!"

Chloe was beautiful and dark blond. I'd mistaken her for a hippie because her blue eyes sparkled like spring rain. Her Canadian accent was barely traceable, and she acted more American than the locals; she'd spent the last two years in New Jersey, so that was probably why.

She asked, "It's Jenny, right?"

"Right. Chloe?"

"Right! That's totally awesome we remembered each other's names. Are you a junior?"

"You know it."

"Me too! Wicked. I got stuck here because all the other housing was full. Gee, what is this place, Woodstock or something?"

"I know, right? My roommate like lives off tofu crackers and bong hits."

"Okay, I might sound stupid right now, but I totally thought you were one of them."

"Me? No way. I was just being quiet."

"Then you like shopping?"

"Hell yes."

"And TCBY?"

"Amen."

"And dating guys without having sex?"

"Chloe, we're gonna get along perfectly."

Chapter FOUR

CHLOE TOTALLY ROCKS

The entire school consisted of about five hundred students, and they were all gathered in the gymnasium. I scanned the crowd for Josh Beck, but he probably wouldn't be back until tomorrow when classes started. In the meantime, Chloe and I looked for no one in particular.

New country. New school. New guys. I was like Dr. Seuss as I counted them off: fat guys, slim guys, nerdy guys, gym guys, big guys, small guys, strong guys, tall guys . . . you get the point.

The school dean took center court with a microphone. "Welcome to Molson Academy! And for those returning, welcome back! I'm Dean Sanders, and I promise you a fun and event-filled year."

He certainly nailed it when he said "event-filled." Anyway, I won't bore you with details. Here's what you need to know:

1. On weekdays there was a ten o'clock curfew. On weekends the curfew was midnight. Housemothers and fathers and resident advisers were responsible for upholding the curfew.

2. You were not allowed outside school grounds for more than two hours without special consent. Security booths were set up at all gates to ensure that you didn't leave without permission.

3. Parties were restricted, as were sleepovers between guys and girls, unless you were a hippie named Jacinda with a hairy boyfriend.

Okay, I added that hippie part. I guess I was just confused as to how Jacinda slept over at her boyfriend's place so often without getting in trouble. Then again, maybe breaking the rules would be easier than I thought.

"God, I totally love those wineglasses," I said. The glasses were on the table next to us. "We should get some of those for our place. It's almost cruel that they have them here—"

"'Cause we're not allowed to drink!" Chloe finished my thought with a strange glee. She was cute like that.

We were eating linner (late lunch/early dinner) that night at Momma Molson's, the campus restaurant, which served killer salads. We'd been there like five times already, and I usually got the Fire-Roasted Veggie Salad add grilled chicken hold the cheese and Chloe the no crispy wonton Asian Chicken Salad dressing on the side. Oh, and we only ordered the half size because ohmigod, they were enough to feed three people.

We sat outside, where the air was still pretty humid, and I felt kinda gross. Chloe didn't seem to care about the heat, though. Then again, she always kind of sported this oblivious gaze, so I could never really tell what she was thinking.

I loved the gaze, though. I loved Chloe. She was fun and really open-minded in her own way. And like me, she came from a well-off family. Her dad owned a company that made laundry machines.

Anyway, Chloe and I had grown much closer in the days following our bathroom encounter. It turned out we even had the same cell phones! We set them to the same ringtone just to be corny. Other than that, we were united by a common love of bargain shopping, soy chai lattes, TCBY, and dating guys.

Speaking of guys, our waiter was adorable. I could see his reflection in Chloe's oversize sunglasses. He was probably a senior, and I could tell he'd already set his sights on my new best friend. And who could blame him? She was totally hot!

Smirking confidently, he poured our waters and chatted us up about the daily specials. I guess Chloe liked him because she ordered his recommendation in lieu of the usual. Personally, I wouldn't have chanced it. The following conversation was so typical for this girl:

Waiter: "And do you want the soup or salad with that?"

Chloe: "Super salad? That sounds too big. I'll just stick with the salmon, thanks."

Waiter: "Well, it's free. The soup is really good, eh. How about it?"

Chloe: "But you said it was a salad. Oh, wait. Oh, oops. Okay, right on. Soup *or* salad. Ummm . . . oh . . . you said the soup was good. Rarrr . . . I'm totally undecided here. Can you choose?"

Waiter: "You got it. What's your name?"

Chloe: "Chloe."

Waiter: "Chloe, that's a real pretty name. I'm Jacques."

Chloe: "Hi, Jacques."

Jacques: "I'll make sure you're happy with what you get."

Chloe: "Wicked. C'est cool, Jacques."

Jacques: ". . ."

Chloe: ". . ."

Me: "Ahem. Jenny."

Jacques: "Yeah, good to meet you, Jenny. I'll put your order in."

He was cute, but his accent was a little heavy and irritating for me.

In those first few weeks there were two common situations where I found myself questioning my choice in leaving home. One was whenever I saw the hairy armpits that infested my precious home. The other was when I heard heavy Canadian accents that made me feel like I'd entered a completely different world, even if my native New York was only hours away. I found myself missing the New York dialect and attitude, even the sarcasm.

I thought of Josh Beck. Couldn't he just get here already?

Jacques walked by and smiled again in Chloe's direction. She seemed lost in her own world, where super salads might have really existed, so I brought us back to reality. "He totally wants you," I said, as if she didn't know.

"What? No way."

"Chloe, are you serious? How much you wanna bet he asks you out?"

"He just wants a nice tip. Ohmigod, Jenny, you look amazing in that shirt. You should keep it." It was hers. We'd raided each other's wardrobes before leaving the house. I was wearing her V-neck sheer navy blouse with Guess jeans, and she my striped tank top with Juicy capris.

"Are you proposing a trade?" I asked.

"How about this: If he asks me out, then you can keep the shirt. Your boobs look totally hot in it."

"What?!"

"I'm serious. I wish I had boobs like yours."

I felt a little awkward, so I didn't respond. Chloe wasn't done, though. "I have a girlfriend in Jersey with boobs like yours. I used to touch them all the time. They were just so fun. I'm not, like, you know, gay or anything, though."

"Really? I always worry they're gonna sag once I have kids."

"Not if you get enough exercise and eat right. I saw this thing about it on the Food Network."

"There was something about boobs on the Food Network?"

"Here you are, my dear." Jacques arrived with Chloe's food. "Soup *and* salad. Now *you* can choose. Bon appetit!"

"Oh that's so nice!"

"Anything for a pretty lady."

"There's no way I'll be able to eat all of this, though."

"Jenny'll help, eh. Say, Chloe, do you have any plans on Thursday?"

I didn't love the shirt or anything, but it was as good as mine!

Later that night we sat in the den pigging out on mini carrots and watching a *Sex and the City* episode on DVD. It was the one where Carrie gets dumped on a Post-it and almost gets arrested the same day. A semi-obvious topic came up.

"Jenny?"

"Yeah."

"Are you a virgin?"

"Yeah. Are you?"

"Yeah. I knew it! Wicked!"

"I guess I just want the first time to be really special, ya know?"

"I had this boyfriend last year. We were together for ten months and he kept begging me, *begging* me, to sleep with him. But I wouldn't because I knew that he wasn't going to be my boyfriend forever. Ya know what I mean? It was like we both totally loved each other but we were never *in* love. God, it always sounded so corny to me when people said that, but it's true. I want my first time to be something I remember when I'm ninety years old."

"I wonder if we'll still know each other."

"We will. Definitely." Chloe's eyes lit up then. "Oh, wait a sec!" She put her oversize Louis Vuitton bag on her lap. "I got you something."

"You did? What?"

She reached in and carefully pulled out two shiny objects: the wineglasses from Momma Molson's. "I bet you forgot."

"Chloe. You totally rock."

Chapter FIVE

PROFESSOR STONE TOTALLY TEACHES

The night before classes Chloe and I went to a back-to-school party held in one of the senior houses. Tagging along were each of our roommates, Jacinda and Orly, who didn't really get along. Somehow Jacinda's obsession with Eastern religions just couldn't coexist peacefully with Orly's devotion to astrology. Personally, I sided with Jacinda, 'cause I thought astrology was like the dumbest thing on the planet, but that's beside the point. I mean, it just cracks me up when you tell someone your sign and they nod as if they suddenly know everything about you . . . but okay, I'll stop now.

The reason we brought the two along was so that they'd make up and eventually agree to room together so that Chloe and I could do the same. It didn't really work out, though, because unbeknownst to Chloe and me, Jacinda had slept with Orly's boyfriend last year. After both girls drank like two beers, Orly just flipped her shit and they both disappeared into the night.

"Thanks a lot, Green!" Jacinda yelled as she took off for God knows where. Jeez, for such lovers of harmony, hippies sure could strike some pretty violent chords.

The hours that followed found us drinking Smirnoff vodka and cranberry and socializing. I asked a cute guy how everyone got away with partying, and it turned out he was the housefather! I guess that pretty much answered everything. *Très* cool.

Anyway, I must have met like fifty new people, and for the first time I truly felt comfortable in my new surroundings. I gave my number to two guys but was secretly hoping they wouldn't call. Josh Beck had first dibs.

The attention was still nice, though. The only annoying thing was when someone wanted to shake your hand because it was always with the right. You're probably thinking I'm, like, a total crackhead for getting peeved over something as little as that, but you know what? It was a big deal. It was always the right hand. Being a lefty can be a pain in the A, FYI. Compared to the hand thing, I was even willing to tolerate the ridiculous kissing on each cheek thing that was French tradition.

The night ended with Chloe and me on the roof of our house, sipping Molson Export beer out of our new wineglasses and listening to my iPod Shuffle. It was super easy to get beer, by the way. All it took was a trip into the city and some cleavage; I didn't even need an ID. And as long as my messenger bag had papers and books on top, the security guard never noticed a forty-ounce Molson Export underneath.

As Lily Allen played, we watched the stars and talked about our futures. Chloe was gonna be a lawyer with a veterinarian husband and two kids. I was gonna be a famous actress married to a brain surgeon, but I wasn't sure how many kids we'd have. It was a killer night.

But the next morning I awoke nervous and bitter. It was the first day of school all over again. I dreaded the usual: failing tests, embarrassing myself in front of the class. How many new people would cross me? How many would I cross?

I debated skipping out to go shopping but figured it wouldn't get things off to the greatest start. I just hoped I didn't make any enemies—I mean, Jacinda was already pretty annoyed with me. It's not like I was scared of her; I just didn't want enemies this early in my boarding-school career. If Jacinda *did* cross me, though, I'd get my revenge. I usually did.

As I dressed I made a mental list of people who'd wronged me in life. In most cases I'd found sweet revenge, although a few got away clean. I never avenged something unless the cause was righteous. I was an extremely fair person.

Here was a partial list I came up with:

1. ARI WEINBERG. Seventh grade. This was in Hebrew school. He stole the cantor's expensive tallis and threw it in the toilet, which let's just say hadn't been flushed in a while. The cantor was my second favorite person in the whole synagogue, and he was literally brought to tears. A tallis is like a sacred Jewish scarf, FYI.

My revenge was ever so sweet. Ari was a slacker, right, and for his bar mitzvah he'd made a little cheat sheet for his Torah reading. It had all the pronunciations and the words written in English letters. *Ba-ruch a-tah.*

To make things even in the eyes of God, I swiped his precious sheet an hour before he led the service. I can still picture Ari's beet red face stuttering the words, sometimes making words up, as the symphony of snickers arose from all his classmates watching. Eventually the rabbi had to escort him from the podium. It was priceless. Cheaters never win, Ari.

2. BENJI BENSON. Fourth grade. Robbed the classroom election from me by taking votes from my ballot box. Trust me, he did it. Here was one I had to wait like an eternity to avenge.

I finally got my chance freshman year of high school, when Benji ran for class president. The position was as good as his, since no one else was even running. Like a tigress, I waited patiently for my kill.

Finally, a week before the election, I put my name on the ballot. I guess I was still cool with everyone then, and with few days to spare I quickly campaigned: I put up posters, I . . . well, I pretty much just put up posters.

But then, on the day of the elections, I arranged for the entire freshman football team to hand-scoop ice cream at a make-your-own-sundae bar that Daddy set up for me in the cafeteria. Everyone loved it.

The truth was, I didn't have to bother with any of it, because I won by a landslide. Benji was devastated. Thanks, Benji: Because of you my college applications would be certified gold. I spent the year planning dances and pushing for more Diet Snapple in the soda machines.

3. DOUG LAPIDUS. The Facebook loser who shared my zit with the World Wide Web; the MySpace addict who blogged about my misfortunes. Getting him back was practically a summer job.

Equipped with photos of an old camp friend, I set up a fake MySpace page using the name Sheila Pace. It took like ten minutes to lure Doug into my trap, and pretty soon we were writing to each other like every day. "Sheila" got him to admit all this weird stuff about himself, like how when he was feeling lonely he talked to his dead insect collection and pretended each dead bug was a different popular guy in school. Gross.

I copied all our conversations and posted links to them on like everyone's respective Facebook walls and MySpace pages. Doug wasn't blogging much after that. Score!

4. VERONICA COHEN. She basically convinced Mark Leibowitz to ask her to prom after he'd already asked me. I had the biggest crush on him too, which she totally knew! My blood reached new temperatures that day. I could've strangled Veronica until her color-changing contacts popped out of her feeble eyes.

I hadn't gotten her back yet, but her day would come. Boy, her day would come. Just thinking about her made me wanna scream.

I headed out the door with Veronica still on my mind. It left me unsettled, as if I'd eaten a giant half salad but was still hungry, or was on some defective colon cleanser diet. Damn you, Cohen!

It was September third and ten in the morning. My first class was AP Calculus. Great, just what I needed.

Remember when I said something about cheating on an entrance exam? Well, I didn't want Daddy to think I wasn't worth the investment, so when they had us take these preliminary math tests, I casually found the dorkiest-looking guy in the room and cheated off his answers. It totally worked!

Okay, okay, I know it's dishonest, but if you'd seen the look on Daddy's face when he found out I got into AP, you would've totally known it was worth it. I just wanted him to be happy.

Now all I had to figure out was how to make it through the year in a super-hard math class. I was pretty smart, though, so I was sure I could pull it off.

Pointing to some weird drawings on the board, the math teacher said in true nerd fashion, "Okay, we'll start off with an easy one:

Given that the line c has the parametric equations $x = 5 - 3t$, $y = -2 + t$, $z = 1 + 9t$; what are the parametric equations for a line through $P(-6, 4, -3)$ and parallel to c? Please feel free to discuss it with one another."

Hmm . . . let's see . . . yeah . . . or maybe I *couldn't* pull it off. I mean, he might as well have been speaking Chinese. I was totally screwed, and all that anxiety I'd worried about climbed into my throat. What had I gotten myself into?

Not even knowing how to plug the equation into my calculator, I just scribbled numbers and symbols on a sheet of paper. I had no F-ing clue what I was doing, but at least I looked busy. I decided that if the teacher called on me, I'd just leave.

"What the hell?" said a Canadian voice behind me. I turned to face like the cutest guy I'd ever seen, cute in that nonsexual nerd way, though. He had ruffled dark hair and dorky glasses, behind which his brown eyes squinted at my made-up math. "What are you doing?"

"Hi . . ."

"Edgar."

"Edgar, I need serious help."

"What am I, a doctor? What's your name?"

"Jenny Green."

"Green. Of Jewish descent, I presume. I thought Jews were supposed to be smart."

"We usually are! I'm just really bad at math."

"A really bad math student in AP Calc. Makes no sense, Jenny.

No sense at all. Here . . ." He wrote out all the math for me. I could have kissed him. "There ya go, Greenie. A freebie."

A flood of relief washed over me. "Thank you so much," I said. "Now can you just tell me what all these symbols mean?"

My second class that day was a very special feature at Molson Academy. It was a college-style lecture called Themes in Modern Poetry and Prose, with a highly regarded professor teaching a class of like a hundred juniors and seniors.

Now before you get all bored hearing about my classes, just give this professor, or *prof* as the locals called them, a chance.

At first I thought I was still wearing my sunglasses. Was it just me or was the lecture hall really dim? I sat toward the front in case the *prof* had a weakness for cute girls.

Suddenly a barrage of colors were projected onto a big screen up front. Music played—it sounded like crazy African drums. The sensory overload almost made me nauseous.

Amidst the light show, a solitary figure advanced quietly from the wings. His head was drooping, as though he were summoning mystic energy or something weird like that.

The crazy colors disappeared from the screen and the music stopped. The figure stood before the class, and through the darkness I could see that his jacket was really old-school plaid. He held a cane by his side.

Finally he looked up and declared, "Did this presentation make you feel awkward? Uncomfortable? Excited? If you answered yes to any or all of those questions, you are in the right place."

His head drooped again. Totally weird. "Lights!" he bellowed. Soon the room was filled with brightness, and we all squinted to adjust.

When my vision finally came into focus, I saw a man who was as much a stereotype as I was. He was the man who would change my life.

I noticed he didn't limp, so what was up with the cane? Who did he think he was, Willy Wonka or something? Then there was the jacket, some checkered brown relic that he'd probably been wearing since the seventies. It had tan elbow patches that were tacky but charming in their own way. It was so college. He had a prickly gray beard and short, unkempt hair. His unyielding eyes were like small rocks.

"I am Prof Stone. I am a student like you. To this day I'm still learning things, like that glue comes from horses. Why didn't I know that? I don't know. But I learned it today; therefore, today I am a learner. I want to learn with you. Will you let me? You will? Good. Now let's cut to the chase. Art!"

Then suddenly he raced forward and put his face right in mine! I mean, he was like centimeters away. It was everything I'd feared!

"What is your name?"

"Jenny Green."

"Jenny Green, does my proximity to your face make you feel uncomfortable?"

"Umm . . . not really?" I lied.

"No? How about now?" He moved in even closer.

Now I was really flustered. "Yes."

"It does? Good. You know what I am? I am art. I am stimulus and you have a response." Thankfully he backed away, and the red left my cheeks. For some reason I didn't feel that embarrassed. Close call.

He boomed, "If art makes you feel very uncomfortable, then it's done its job—it's elicited a response. I'd rather you passionately hate the material we'll be reading than merely dislike it. I'd rather make you queasy than make you bored. Sex and death, religion, emotion, more sex, more death. These topics might make you squirm, but that's how we know they're important. Lights!"

The lights dimmed. A projection appeared on the big screen behind him: a pretty young woman. Professor Stone pointed his cane. "This is Mrs. Stone. My second wife. We have sex. Lots of it." And as he said this, he put his cane at his groin and thrust it toward the screen. Half the class was laughing hysterically. I could hardly breathe.

"I love her . . . not just because of the sex, but the companionship and the trust. I would die if it meant saving her life, but during arguments there's no one on the planet I'd rather kill. Why? The texts we read in this class might help us answer that question."

He talked with such power and confidence. Another guy up

there could say the same exact thing and sound just plain nuts. But there was something about *Prof* Stone that made me giddy for more.

Now, I wasn't the biggest reader. I went through this Patricia Highsmith phase last year, but in most cases I'd rather catch the movie. With Prof Stone, though, I was sure I'd make the effort.

Veronica Cohen could have Mark Leibowitz and prom. I had Themes in Modern Poetry and Prose. I shuddered deeply in my seat.

Chapter SIX

JOSH KIND OF ROCKS

It proved fairly easy to track down Josh Beck. Some random girl knew him and said he was usually at the school gym around five.

Okay, I'm totally gonna sound like a stalker now, but I basically camped outside the gym until I spotted Josh. It was worth the wait, though, because at six o'clock he exited the preppy brick building. He was more handsome than I even remembered, and having just come from a workout, there was an extra special sexiness to him.

It had to be perfect. After gaining an idea of where he was headed, I secretly ran parallel to him, using some trees as a cover. When I reached a good point I stopped, turned, and walked casually in his direction. Kind of psycho, I know, but he was totally coming my way!

I played it cool and didn't look at him. I probably should've, though, because somehow we smacked right into each other. Nice going, Jenny!

"Whoa, look out!" he said.

"Sorry."

"Jenny?"

"Josh?"

"Holy shit. What the hell are you doing here?"

"Going to school, duh."

"I go to school here!"

"Oh my God. That is so cool."

"Cool? It's incredible! I can't believe this. We're hanging out."

It was that easy. He was gonna stop by at eight on Friday and we'd grab a bite at Momma Molson's and then take it from there. Ohmigod! Josh Beck!!!

It was Friday and I was back in Prof Stone's lecture. My date with Josh was that night, but it was another man I focused on for the time being.

Maybe I was imagining things, but I swear to this day that the professor looked directly at me every time he talked about sex.

"In case you couldn't tell, I'm a firm supporter of fornication," he said. "As we all know, sex is affirmation and destruction. It's experimentation. It's a journey, except unlike most journeys this one has a definite destination. The big O. Give me an O yeah!" Some of the guys actually did this. Gross.

Suddenly an overwhelming feeling of embarrassment came

over me and I began to blush. I cursed my mother quietly for giving me such sensitive, blushing skin.

I'll confess something now. I wasn't just a virgin. At that time I had yet to achieve an orgasm. I sort of thought I had one the summer before with this NYU grad student Andy Harris but realized it was just wishful thinking.

Anyway, it was like sophomore year all over again. Prof Stone had said, "As we all know" and I didn't know! I wanted to know!

The professor continued, "It amazes me the utterly titanic amount of human history that's governed by some guy who was out looking for that O. But you know why he was looking? Because it's a moment of clarity among a species overburdened by bullshit. Hence the connection between sex and death arises. Like sex, death is climactic. Or better phrased, like death, sex is climactic."

I realize that age sixteen is no age to be fretting over sex, but sometimes if you read one too many *Cosmo*s or watch one too many episodes of *Grey's Anatomy* you can't help but feel you're totally missing out on something. Would Josh Beck help me find it?

Not if I had anything to do with it . . .

For those of you to whom this has happened, you're not alone. For those of you laughing: One day it'll happen to you. Trust me.

It was Friday night at 7:48. I'm a girl who likes to be well prepared. Preparation takes at least an hour and a half, but I'd only given myself an hour because there was this killer episode of *Friends* on and I lost track of time. So I showered at 6:50 and blow-dried my hair. I didn't style it yet or put on any makeup, because I always waited until I was dressed.

I left the bathroom at seven fifteen. Now what, you ask, had I been doing between seven fifteen and now? I'd been pacing the hallway in my wife beater and boxer shorts, that's what, because my door was locked and Jacinda was off camping or something. She must have literally left the second I turned on the shower. I bet she planned it that way, that stupid hippie! Anyway, inside my room was the new shirt from Nordstrom's with matching pants just sitting on my bed. I needed to get to those clothes!

Now those of you thinking, *Jenny, just borrow something from Chloe! Hurry up!* Well, too little too late, because Chloe was on a second date with stupid Jacques (I didn't care for Jacques much) and her door was locked too. It left me with one option and one option only.

It was ten minutes and counting. Having decided once and for all what needed to be done, I knocked on the door right next to ours: Olivia's. She was that weirdo with the shaved rainbow head and I could hear her playing that annoying clarinet.

I knocked again, louder this time, muttering, "C'mon, you F-ing Pied Piper, there's no time for this BS!" I had a date with Josh Beck and he was gonna think I was a total flake. I'd answer the door in my shit gear and he'd turn around and leave. Or better yet, I'd be forced to borrow clothes from one of the hippies and answer the door wearing a tie-dye and Birkenstocks. Which way to the PETA rally?

I knocked again. LOUDLY. "Olivia, please open up, this is an emergency!"

Finally the clarinet ceased and the door swung open. Olivia, who was pretty chunky, especially for a vegan, stood before me. I could never understand how she managed to shave her head all the time but miss her armpits.

Anyway, she was not pleased. "What?" she growled. "Can't you hear I'm trying to practice, Jenny?"

"Olivia, this is serious. I have a major date in five minutes and I can't get to my clothes."

"So . . . you wanna borrow something?"

Yeah, right, I thought. "Uh . . . not exactly. You have to let me use your window."

"The window?"

"Yes, I'm going to crawl out and scale the ledge. I leave my window unlocked, so I should be able to get into my room."

"Are you crazy?"

Crazy or not, it's what I did.

Olivia's dirty window swung open into the cool night. It was only a two-story drop, but still I would've totally broken something. I shuffled onto the very small ledge and gripped the wall for dear life.

Holding on to whatever stone I could, I inched my way over to my room. From the street came the shouts and calls. "Hey, baby, need a hand?" "Look, it's Spider-Woman!" "Oh my God, she's gonna jump to her almost death!" Very funny, guys. I just prayed that somehow Josh wasn't among them. If he were, I might as well jump.

I won't amplify the story by having my foot slip off the ledge or something, but it was scary enough, okay? The window was in reach. This was the worst part. Maintaining my balance, I had to kneel down and grip the bottom of the frame.

Got it. I pulled. But it wouldn't budge! I pulled harder. Nothing. Stupid window! I was nearly in tears by this point. Refusing to have come this far just to fail, I pulled once more and voilà! Success! Yes! Yes! Yes!

I scurried into my room and into my clothes. The clock read 7:59. Maybe Josh would be late.

DING-DONG!

Shit. Shit shit shit. Well, at least Josh was punctual. In a whirlwind I applied deodorant and styled my hair.

Thankfully, someone let Josh in: Amber. Right then and there I took back all those bad things I wrote about her in that e-mail to Mom. She called up, "Jenny, you have a visitor!"

"I'll be right down!"

It bought me some time. I applied eyeliner and just a tad of blush. Okay, and just a smidgeon of foundation, 'cause I had this little pimple that wasn't going away and it was right next to my nose and . . . okay, okay. I didn't have time for anything else, so I rushed downstairs to greet my handsome prince.

He stood in the doorway, wearing Gap as always. It was so cute how he was so clueless as to what I'd just gone through. And maybe it was all the running and shuffling, but I'd like to think it was him that took my breath away. He was more handsome than ever.

We hugged and kissed each other on the cheek. Josh was delighted to see me. "Hey there! Wow, you look beautiful."

"Stop."

"I'm serious. You look great."

"You too. Are you ready?"

"Well, yeah, but there's just one problem."

"What's wrong?" I asked.

"You're not wearing any shoes."

We were out to dinner, and I was still recovering from the shoe fiasco when I realized I'd totally forgotten my wallet. I was such a klutz. I swear it wasn't intentional. I was just in such a hurry that I'd left the wallet on my dresser.

Now, on a normal date this wouldn't be a problem, but this wasn't a normal date; it wasn't necessarily a date at all. After all, I was sitting at Momma Molson's and next to my Fire-Roasted Veggie Salad (add chicken hold the cheese) was a big laptop computer. That's right, folks, a big Macintosh laptop filled with pictures of Josh's "buddies." He wouldn't shut up about it.

"Mac kills the competition. See this feature here? I can add things to their faces. Wanna see my buddy Weebo with a mustache? I can draw it in! Cool, huh?"

It's kind of funny how your image of someone can be so completely disrupted in a matter of seconds (and no, I'm not talking about Weebo with a mustache). Thank God his iPhone was in the shop.

Oh, and I didn't even mention the best part. Josh wasn't Jewish! I figured this out when he ordered the prosciutto and melon appetizer.

"You're not kosher?" I asked. I wasn't kosher either, but whatever.

He furled his brow. "Why the hell would I be kosher? Being kosher's not kosher."

"You're not Jewish?"

"Is that a problem?"

"Of course not. It's just I thought everyone from high school was Jewish or Persian. And even the Persians were Jewish."

"Don't be so judgmental," he said. Great, he didn't even have a sense of humor. It made me want to cry. I'd schlepped all the way to Canada for nothing.

Fortunately, Josh redeemed himself come dessert. My raspberry parfait was placed before me, and I couldn't help but say something totally girly. "I shouldn't have ordered this."

"What? Are you serious? You're so pretty, though. It won't hurt, trust me."

"You're just saying that."

"No way, Jenny. You're perfect. I can't wait to see more of you. I'm gonna show you all the best places. Things here get pretty wild, ya know what I mean?"

Okay, he was still a nerd and sure, his "wild" times probably involved three of his "buddies," a bottle of Malibu rum, and high-speed Internet connections, but it was that last part that really hooked me; the "ya know what I mean" part, because the way he said it was just like home.

When the check came, Josh dropped his card. I grabbed my purse as if I wasn't yet aware there was no money in it, but he waved me off. "Don't even think about it," he said. Then he slammed his computer shut, and like every negative experience from dinner vanished into the lethargic night air.

We took a long stroll (sorry, I like the word "stroll") and talked about things besides Macintosh. I grew fonder of Josh. It was a relief to find out he was a hardcore Yanks fan and not just a tech nerd, and slowly he morphed back into the handsome, funny guy all of us girls admired in junior high.

While Josh lived in the city with his parents, he knew Molson well enough to give me a brief tour of all the cool spots. First there was Molson Tower. It was this tall, abandoned bell tower right next to Science Hall. I'd seen it earlier but hadn't really thought about it. The tower was really old-school, and Josh showed me a secret by wedging a credit card in the door, which swung open. He asked if I wanted to walk up, but it looked pretty creepy inside, so I passed.

Next he showed me Lover's Lounge. I'd never seen anything like it. It was in the basement of the Social Studies Building, where the students had totally revamped some storage space into a private hangout with lava lamps, music, etc. We cuddled on a fluorescent beanbag chair.

"There's no way the school doesn't know about this," I said.

"Molson's cool like that," Josh assured me. He pecked me on the forehead—it was actually kind of strange. Then he said, "I really like you, Jenny."

"Really?" Why? I wondered.

"You're funny. You're smart, too."

"Smart enough to forget my shoes."

"See, that was funny! When can we hang out next?"

Before I could even answer, he planted a big wet one on my lips. Well, that's kind of hamming it up—it was more like we both stuck our tongues down each other's throats. Anyway, it was my first kiss at boarding school, and even though it was poorly timed, it was still pretty good.

We made out for a while, and then he walked me home. When I closed the door behind me, I leaned against it like I was that girl in the movies who'd just fallen for the perfect guy. I knew I hadn't necessarily fallen and Josh was far from perfect, but just let me have my moment, okay?

I went upstairs and grabbed my phone. For some strange reason I felt like calling Daddy and convincing him to buy me a Mac.

Chapter SEVEN

TERROR SEX

It was mid-September, and my new life in Montreal had been running smoothly. With help from Edgar I was getting by in math, and with help from Prof Stone I was actually enjoying my education. Chloe and Jacques were dating, and Chloe and I were closer than ever. I'd adjusted to the house, too. Some of the hippies even offered me brownies (but their smile was a little too eager, so I politely refused).

That's not to mention Josh. While he was still far from the McDreamy I thought he'd be, we still had a pretty good time together. He even put flirtatious messages on my Facebook wall for everyone to see! Read it and weep, Long Island. Oh, and you won't believe it, but he actually told me the password to his Mac desktop! Pssst, it's "Galaxy8."

On the weekends I spent two hours at a time at his parents' place in the city. Because Josh didn't live on campus, he had special permission to come and go, but unfortunately, that didn't extend to me. It was *très* cool walking around Montreal with a seasoned resident like Josh, though, even if we had to stop in a computer store like twice a day. I was truly beginning to feel at home.

Then, on September tenth, came the worst news you could ever imagine. . . .

"Students and faculty alike were shocked when a junior here at Molson Academy was arrested earlier this morning on conspiracy charges. Acting on a tip, police rushed into the suspect's room, where they found a box of semiautomatic handguns and a list of students he planned to execute in yet another school shooting."

That was on the news. The hippies, weirdos, Chloe, and I all watched in the den with our mouths agape. It was the first we'd heard of it.

As the day progressed, more information surfaced. His name was Harrison Bennett, and he was in my AP Calc class. To be honest, I had no recollection of the guy, which in a class of fifteen is saying a lot. Apparently he was American, born and raised in Minnesota. Needless to say, AP was canceled for that week.

Later that afternoon I was called in to meet Dean Sanders himself.

"Hello, Jenny. It's a pleasure to meet you, and we're thrilled to have you here at Molson. It's a terrible occurrence what happened on campus today, and the entire administration is shaken. The reason we called you here is because we feel it's important that you have certain privileged information. It's about the list Harrison made."

"What about it?"

"There were quite a few students on it . . . and you were one of them. We're obligated to tell you, and we hope it's not too soon. We just want to be straightforward with our students. Please don't let this intimidate you too much. This kind of thing is a rarity in Canada. The boy won't be anywhere near here for a long time. He was American, you know."

It was almost a cheap shot the way he said it; as if only Americans were capable of school shootings. But there was a school shooting at some junior college in Montreal a few years ago. I remembered it. It wasn't just an American epidemic anymore.

"We have a counselor on campus. His name's Mr. Carr, and he's there whenever you need him, Jenny. Jenny?"

I was frozen stiff. Memories flooded my feeble mind—memories of 9/11. My family and I were supposed to go into the city the night before to watch a Broadway play and stay at a hotel. It was a tradition. We called them "Green Apple Nights," and Daddy let us take off from school and everything.

Anyway, Daddy had a friend in the towers that we were going to visit the morning of 9/11, and the only reason it didn't happen is because Abby got food poisoning and everything was canceled. Daddy's friend died in the attacks. It took me years to recover from the fact that I, too, almost died that day. And here death was again, knocking on the door but not coming inside. It chilled me to my core. What the F was up with September?

"Dean Sanders?" I said.

"Yes? What is it? Anything."

"Can I have special permission to go off campus tonight for more than two hours?" It was all I could really think of. I had a date at Josh's place.

I left Dean Sanders feeling angry at first. I felt angry that society had created these sociopathic maniacs who couldn't make friends and wanted everyone to suffer for it. It made me so angry I could've killed someone myself.

But as day turned to night the anger subsided, giving way to one thing only: fear. My boiling blood had turned cold. I was alone in a foreign land, and my life was a fragile flame that could be blown out—just like that. Not even the sound of my mother's voice could put me at ease. In fact, it did the exact opposite, since she was like flipping out. Whatever.

I don't know when summer ended that year, but for me that day marked the beginning of fall. There was just suddenly this gloomy autumn chill in the air that even global warming couldn't change.

So I was like totally scared. I can't even tell you how many paranoid thoughts popped into my head, but by dusk there was only one worry left: my virginity. Sure, it was precious, but what good was it if you took it to your grave? I totally didn't want to die a virgin, it wasn't fair.

Shivering, I looked around and realized I'd been walking since noon. It was almost six o'clock now. I was supposed to be at Josh's by seven.

I thought of Prof Stone and that world of sexual knowledge he always paraded before us with his poetry and stupid acrobatics. I thought of Samantha in *Sex and the City*. I was tired and afraid of not being in that world. I wanted to know the touch that was so commonplace to so many. It was advertised daily, it made up half the conversation among students (at least it felt that way); it was the line dividing Jenny the girl from Jenny the woman.

I couldn't die having never achieved what I'd spent so long working toward. Maybe it didn't have to be perfect, it just had to be. It just had to be.

I raced home to change and then headed into the city. I was at Josh's by seven thirty.

"I'm sorry," I said in the doorway. "I'm . . . sorry."

"What's wrong?"

Then I just broke down. It was all too much. I told Josh everything. He squeezed me tight and told me it would be okay and that he'd take care of me. It was the sweetest he'd been to me.

By the time he poured my first glass of wine, I just wanted to forget everything.

And forget things we did.

Josh's parents were out for the night and it was just the two of us. I had special permission from the dean himself to be off campus for the night as long as I kept my housemother posted. I'd even turned off my cell phone for the occasion.

The smell of chicken Marsala filled the apartment, and like

some aphrodisiac it carried me away. From the kitchen, Josh cooked. He wore this hilarious apron that said FUCK THE COOK on it. While the sauce simmered, he poured me some more wine, and with each new glass the night grew more and more enchanting.

He'd gone all out. The table was set with flowers and candles, and for dinner he brought out another bottle of red wine. This one was really expensive and like aged more than a bubbie in Florida. And I'm not usually the biggest chicken Marsala fan, but Josh swore I'd love it and I totally did, I think (I was kinda drunk by that point).

"Josh, this is so good."

"You like? I knew you were lactose intolerant, so I made my best nondairy dish. I'm so glad it pleases the lady. You know, Jenny, I think about you all the time. I want more of you. I want to watch movies until sunrise. I want to just hold you. It sounds cliché, I know."

"No, it doesn't. It sounds affectionate."

"Well, I'm not used to it. You bring it out of me."

He was being so totally sweet, and the food was so good. Everything was perfect until I heard a familiar noise emanate from his room. "Oh shit," Josh said casually as he stood. "I'll be right back." It was his stupid computer—I knew it. Well, at least he didn't put it on the table.

I almost ate my words as Josh came back into the room, holding his precious Mac ever so carefully. He rested it on the kitchen counter where he could keep an eye on it, then sat back down.

"Downloading something," was all he offered by way of explanation. I felt a tinge of nausea and took a big gulp of wine.

By the time dinner was over, I was pretty wasted. Maybe that was part of Josh's plan, because he seemed like totally sober. Anyway, it wasn't long before he and I were on the couch and it wasn't long after being on the couch that Josh was on top of me.

In my woozy head I knew it was time. Dinner had been so ideal, sort of. Josh was so sweet and tall and handsome, I guess. He wasn't Jewish, but it didn't matter really. I never said I was gonna marry the first guy I had sex with. Besides, who's to say Josh wouldn't convert or something if need be?

So he slipped his hands up my shirt and I did the same to him. We were both topless in the course of a few deep kisses. He said nothing, only nodded toward the bedroom. I nodded back.

The butterflies were beating ferociously in my stomach, but the wine helped sedate them. I swear it sounds corny, but that cheesy prom song by Eric Clapton was playing in my head. You know: "You look wonderful tonight . . ." For a second Prof Ston replaced Eric Clapton, and I giggled at the thought of my cor professor singing.

"What is it?" Josh asked. We were sitting on his bed nov

"Nothing."

"You're really beautiful, Jenny."

"Am I?"

"I want to know you."

So cheesy, right? But at the time it sounded re

_te._

5

Thinking it would be sexy, I didn't respond—I merely pulled at his belt, unbuckling it.

Suddenly he was way too excited, but so was I. As I unbuttoned my jeans, he reached into a drawer. Nice, I didn't need to ask if he had a condom. I slid off my pants and breathed nervously. So this was it. The moment I'd been waiting for. Ohmigod, I was gonna lose my virginity!

All right, Josh, let's see what you're made of. He eased me back against the semi-soft mattress. Okay, okay. He kissed me all over. Nice. And then he was inside me. There wasn't much pain, more like discomfort as he pumped away. Then for a brief moment there was a flash of great pleasure. More, more, more. I wanted more.

Josh thrust his hips. Yes! It felt good. He thrust them again. Yes! Yes! He thrust them for the last time, then pulled out and released a groan of ecstasy before I'd barely gasped.

Wait. That was it? What the F was that?

Josh collapsed onto my shoulder like a fallen giant. I could el the sweat from his forehead all over my tender skin. Then I snelled something weird. Was that Vaseline?

Whatever. It was over. It was over and it was awful.

"You liked that?" he asked.

"Sure. You wanna maybe do it again?"

No way. I'm pooped."

d there was something about that word: "pooped." And ing about the knowledge that I'd just given away my most ossession to a guy that used the word "pooped."

The nausea swelled. The butterflies all wanted to vomit. I wanted to leave. Instead I just lay there beneath his big, lousy body wondering how I'd tell Chloe. It was then I noticed something.

"Hey, you didn't take the condom off."

"I never put it on."

"What?"

"Condoms and vaginas don't mix."

"Then what was in the drawer?"

"Vaseline. It's like a lube."

"Eww. Are you serious?"

"Shhh . . . calm down. Don't worry. I didn't cum inside you. Now let's go to bed. In the morning I'll make us French toast."

Hooray. French toast. Come to think of it, the chicken Marsala hadn't been that good.

And that was the story of how I lost my virginity. It's not even its own chapter.

The next morning I awoke in his arms feeling like a prisoner. It's not even accurate to say I awoke, since I'd been up all night, but you catch my drift. The point was, I felt like a statistic. The world I was so eager to join was a cold one. It was a world where men came before women, pun intended.

It was September 11, 2007. I imagined how many women died on this fatal day years ago and how few women would ever steal a plane and crash it into a building.

Meanwhile, Josh was rousing from his slumber. He kissed my

forehead with dry lips. "So, wanna do it again?" he asked. I almost threw up right there on the bed.

"I thought we were gonna have French toast," was all I could think to say.

"You're serious? You don't wanna?"

"Not really."

"Fine then," he said bitterly. "Let's make some fucking French toast." With that he leaped out of bed and went straight to his computer. I could tell he was angry. He didn't face me when he spoke. "It's not fucking fair. You can be so spoiled, Jenny."

"How am I spoiled?"

"You just always get things your way or no way at all."

"Because I don't feel like having sex at eight in the morning? I'm not a morning person!"

"Just forget it. Let me finish this and I'll make your fucking breakfast."

The French toast was too eggy, and the few bites I ate tasted like Vaseline. I could hardly look at Josh without getting sick.

I finally got home around noon. I thought I'd never leave Josh's place. He was like really determined to have sex again. But the thing was, in my head I'd kind of disqualified the whole event. I mean, it was so short it didn't have to count, right?

What I mean is, Josh and I were obviously through, and assuming I wasn't pregnant or didn't have an STD, then it was practically like it never happened. Oh God, I didn't even wanna think about STDs. I'd have to get tested. My Jewish neurosis simply wouldn't allow room for error. I went on this whole imaginative journey of my life with AIDS that I won't get into. All I'll say is if it turned out I had something, I would make sure Josh suffered for it somehow. And what if he'd gotten some inside me? I couldn't be pregnant. Not yet!!

My imaginary STD and pregnancy only made me angrier and angrier with Josh. Whether I liked it or not, I'd been initiated into a new phase of being. I could lie about it, sure, but the truth remained: I'd lost my V-card. I was no longer a V-card-carrying member.

I trudged into my room and plopped down on my bed. My ringtone blared in my ears. I knew it was him. I didn't answer. The door was partially open, and someone pushed it forward. Chloe.

"Ohmigod, Jenny, where have you been?" She was practically in tears. "I've been calling you."

"Chloe, I lost my V-card."

"But Valentine's Day isn't until February."

"No, Chloe. My virginity."

She sat down on the bed next to me. "No," was all she could mutter. It was like she knew. She knew it'd been awful.

"I don't know why I did it, Chlo. I think I was . . . scared of dying a virgin."

It turned out that it happened all the time. I Googled "sex" and "fear" and found a *Time* magazine article talking about it: "Terror Sex." I guess I wasn't the only girl who'd freaked out about dying a virgin. Now I wasn't a virgin, and I wished I were dead.

Chloe rubbed my back. Finally she asked, "How was it?"

"Awful."

"Did you have an orgasm?"

"Not even close."

"Jenny, I hate men."

"Let's not get carried away."

"Fine, I don't hate men, but I hate Jacques. I broke up with him."

"You did? Why, Chloe?"

"All he wanted was sex. It's all they ever want."

"I hate Josh."

"I hate Josh too."

"I thought Jacques was a total loser."

"Let's make a pact. We'll only date guys we both approve of, eh."

"C'est cool, Chloe. Deal. So that means it's over with Jacques and Josh?"

"Jacques and Josh. It sounds like *they* should be together." We laughed, and it made us both feel better.

So Josh was history. At least that's what I thought. The phone rang again.

This was the text conversation between Josh and me on Wednesday:

Josh: your new facebook pictures r pretty awful

Me: thanx josh, can u go away now?

Josh: can u just tell me y u take such stupid pictures?

Me: what the f josh

Josh: what the f. the word is fuck jenny. what the fuck. answer
   my question though

Me: what question?

Josh: why are ur pictures so gay?

Me: fuck off

Josh: don't get so mad jenny. i'm not insulting u personally.
   i'm just saying ur pictures r stupid

Me: ok macdaddy

Josh: dumb jewish bitch

Josh: my gchat name is cool

Me: well since ur obviously not a mack, i can only assume it refers
   to the constant masturbation u perform in front of ur mac.

Josh: what do you mean i'm not a mack? i got u in bed didn't i

Me: lot of good that did me

Josh: what the fuck does that mean? why don't you return
   my calls?

Me: bye josh

Josh: wait. call me jenny!

This is where things got *really* complicated.

It was Friday night, and I was doing homework for biology.
I wore a pink T-shirt and Juicy shorts. There was some sort of
concert at Molson Theatre (in Canada it's spelled the European
way), and Hippie Hall was so quiet that if you listened closely
you could hear Sasha chanting a mantra in her bedroom. I
swear, besides her there was like no one else home.

So there I was, doing my boring homework. To help make it slightly less boring, I put on my iPod. Soon Cyndi Lauper's "Time After Time" filled the room and gave a sort of dark mood to everything. Maybe it's just my memory, but I swear the room had this dismal glow to it, and the way the curtains drifted in the night wind . . . it was all very spooky.

My door was closed. When the knob turned, I noticed but just assumed it was Jacinda. It wasn't. It was Josh. He was wearing Roots sweatpants and he looked totally wasted. Yes, he was carrying his laptop in a black computer bag. He was such a loser! I killed the music.

"What the F are you doing here?"

"The front door was unlocked. You shouldn't do that. You never know who'll just walk right in."

"Yeah, a huge creep just walked in right now."

"Ouch. Still a bitch, I see." Then he reached right out and squeezed my boob.

"Okay, you have to leave now."

"Wait!" he shouted. "Just . . . wait. I came for a reason." He closed the door behind him, gently placed his computer bag on my desk, and came toward me again, with a look in his eyes like he wanted something from me.

I was getting scared. I told him, "Josh, I think you're drunk. Whatever it is, just send me an e-mail. I don't wanna call the cops."

"Jenny, just one more chance." Again he reached for my boob, but I swatted his hand this time.

"Go away, Josh."

"Just give me one more chance."

"I'm calling the cops."

I reached for the phone but Josh, being twice my size, ripped it from my hands. "You're not listening!" he shouted. "Just give me one more chance!"

"Get out of here before I scream!"

I should've just screamed, but whatever. Before I could do anything, he cupped my mouth and tackled me onto Jacinda's multicolored futon. I could smell the liquor on his breath. I think it was Jack Daniels or something. All I could see were his bloodshot eyes filled with rage.

Then he punched me in the stomach. I'd never felt anything like it. The tears covered my face and my heart was beating like an espresso machine on overdrive. I couldn't believe it, but this jerk was trying to rape me.

He punched me again, this time in the ear, causing a high-pitched ring that killed worse than period cramps after you'd skipped a month. Then he let go of my mouth and grabbed my neck, cutting off my voice but not entirely choking me.

I cursed myself for wearing those Juicy shorts, because it was so easy for him to reach down and slide them right off. This was really happening.

I entered a dark world then. A black hole. I sank into a pit where the name Jenny Green meant nothing to me. She was a memory, a ghost of some past I might have lived. She was dead.

In her place was a defenseless animal that needed to somehow survive. A very angry animal.

Josh pushed his palm into my face. I was losing consciousness. I had to figure something out fast. I tried kicking, but the weight of his body pinned my legs to the futon. I flailed my arms but they didn't seem to go anywhere, like they were stuck in ooze. Josh was pulling down his sweatpants.

The panic was unbearable. His pants were at his ankles and he started thrusting at me. I reached out again, this time for something to use. My small hands found it and wrapped around the hard glass: Jacinda's bong. I gripped it and swung as hard as I could.

SMASH! I nailed Josh right in the face. He squealed loudly. It was enough to stop everything, but I didn't stop. Instead I kept stabbing him with the broken bong, piercing his face and throat.

Now, I hate blood, so I won't go into too much detail, but let's just say there was lots of it. For a moment it seemed like nothing else existed but Josh Beck's ugly blood.

His eyes bulged as he pawed wildly at his throat. He made these awful choking noises that again I don't really wanna talk about. I shoved him off me then and scurried to a corner of the room, where I stood watching. I bit my nails at record speed while Josh writhed and squirmed on the futon.

Then he stopped writhing and squirming. He stopped doing anything at all. He just lay there, motionless.

Josh Beck was like totally dead.

Chapter EIGHT

A MILLION AND ONE REASONS WHY I DIDN'T CALL THE COPS

mong those reasons, the most shallow and irrational were:

1. I really, really didn't want my parents finding out I'd lost my virginity.

2. I knew a cop on Long Island and he was a total jerk.

3. My hair was really gross, and what if there was a cute cop?

The most genuine and rational were:

1. There was a chance they wouldn't believe me, and I'd be totally screwed.

2. If everyone found out what happened, I'd probably have to take the year off.

3. We read this book *The Stranger* in school the year before.

Let me explain that last reason. In that book this guy totally shoots someone in self-defense, but instead of just firing once he fires like four times or something. Anyway the police find the act malicious, even though it was self-defense and the main character gets completely screwed. PS, I hadn't actually read the book, but I remembered my teacher talking about it.

I really couldn't determine how many times I'd jabbed the broken glass bong into Josh's neck. It could've been five, it could've been fifty. The truth was, in the heat of the moment I'd grown so mad that for all I knew I could've ripped his head off and forgotten I'd done it.

Last but not least there was the secret reason, and the source of many problems to come: I *wanted* to get away with it. Beneath the anger and the self-defense lay something primal, something pleasurable even. As I'd watched Josh squirm, a feeling came over me I can only describe now as empowerment. Watching this creep die suddenly filled me with a force I'd never known myself to possess. It was all mine. I was Supergirl.

Dwelling on this and much more, I sat in my room. And waited. For the first hour I did nothing, just stared at his corpse. Then by the time everything registered, I figured it was too late to call the cops even if I wanted to. They'd want to know why I'd waited so long.

Chloe would be home soon, so I locked the door. I merely prayed the concert was still going on and the hippies and weirdos were busy tripping or rolling or painting themselves or whatever it was they did.

First I dealt with the body. He'd stopped bleeding, but to be safe I wrapped old T-shirts around his neck and face.

I thanked God (and Daddy) for the big ugly duffel bag then. Who knew it would come to the rescue? I mean, I'd finally found a good use for it besides making me look totally out of whack with today's luggage standards. It was just big enough to fit Josh's huge mass, and don't ask me how, but after an hour I finally squeezed him into it.

The whole time I was running on strength that you couldn't build at the gym. It came from somewhere deep, deep inside me.

Chloe knocked then. I froze. I didn't breathe. She knocked again, calling my name. Finally she left. One minute later she tried my cell. A shrill ringtone echoed once into the quiet night, and I scurried over and quickly pressed the end button. I was so mad at myself for not putting it on silent you have no idea. After waiting a little longer, I went back to work.

The next problem was all the blood, glass, and smelly water. The glass was easy; I picked it up and threw it into the duffel bag. The water was easy too, since most of it was on Josh's clothes.

The blood was a little more difficult. There was a lot of blood.

I really hated blood. I wanted it out of sight ASAP. The fortunate thing is that only some of it had gotten on the futon, and most of it was on Josh's face and clothes. Of course there was some on the floor and it was all still a major problem, but it wasn't as bad as I originally thought.

The futon was the biggest issue. I could come up with only one solution. Knowing how absentminded Jacinda was, I simply flipped the futon and swore to myself I'd buy her a new one later. She'd never know the difference.

What she would notice, however, was the missing bong. I'd tell her I tripped over it and then buy her a new one of those as well. She was a hippie, like how mad could she get?

With the body stuffed in a duffel bag and the mattress flipped, there was just the remaining blood on the floor. In order to clean this, I had to sneak into the kitchen for supplies. Some people were home by this point, so like a ninja I crept covertly through the halls, bolting past open doors and crawling behind sofas.

I was lucky no one saw me, 'cause when I got back to my room I finally noticed that my shirt and shorts were covered in blood.

Then I looked up and saw something much worse: Orion, Raven's dog. He was in the middle of my room, lapping the blood up off the floor! It was so gross I wanted to scream. I mean, I totally, totally hated blood. Bad dog!

His mouth was red from all the you-know-what, so I grabbed my spray bottle and a towel and, closing my eyes, gave him a quick wash. When I opened them again most of the red was gone, but some remained. It wasn't enough to notice, and I had more important things to do.

"Orion, shoo! Shoo!" How had I not locked the door? In fact, where was my key?

As I tried to push Orion out the door, all the while doing my best not to touch his grimy coat of fur and dirt, I simultaneously searched the room desperately for the key. I found it still in the doorknob.

I was totally losing it. I kicked Orion into the hall, then shut and locked the door behind him.

Of course, being a big stupid dog he scratched at the door, and it was like driving me nuts. What if Raven showed up? Stop scratching, you stupid dog! I almost yelled. Then he did stop scratching. Thank God. I checked the door again to make sure it was locked, then I turned back to the floor.

Well, at least Orion helped me with the cleaning. There was less blood now. I hoped he wouldn't get sick.

Anyway, I used my already corroded shirt and shorts to help clean the remaining blood off the floor—a process that turned out to be like almost impossible—then slipped into new clothes. A quick Windex-and-towel job finished off our beautiful hardwood, and believe it or not, everything looked pretty normal after that. It was a shame I'd lose that shirt and shorts—they totally matched, and I hated ruining good clothes—but obviously I had bigger problems to deal with.

I painted my nails, applied eyeliner, and waited more. I guess

I should've showered, but I didn't dare leave the room. Thank God Jacinda didn't come home. She must have been staying at her boyfriend's.

I waited until three in the morning and then put on my cheapest pair of gloves. I didn't want to use expensive ones, 'cause I was gonna throw them away. Then I tied back my hair and put a cheap snow hat over it. If I learned anything from watching all those episodes of *Law & Order*, it was not to leave fingerprints or hairs behind. Oh wait, now there'd be hair on the gloves! And what about the hat? There'd be hair all over the hat! So I put on an extra hat and an extra pair of cheap gloves, and three pairs of socks. Sometimes an endless wardrobe really comes in handy.

I prepared to finalize my crime. Consuming me this whole time was intense energy that never wavered, the same pulse-pounding thrill of superhuman strength in a world of victims. First I snuck back into the kitchen and took a bunch of glass bottles out of recycling. I went back to my room and tossed them into the duffel bag—you'll find out why in a minute. Finally I entered the hall with the duffel bag. Then at the last second I spotted Josh's computer bag and threw it over my shoulder. Really, who brings their laptop to a rape?

How did I carry a two-hundred-pound body, plus the glass bottles, plus the computer, you ask? Well, ask God, or a scientist, because I'll be damned if I know. But I did, and in retrospect it didn't even seem that hard.

I exited the brownstone. The night was chilly and silent. In the distance I saw a flashlight, but it was pointed in another direction.

I was careful to creep behind big buildings and through patches of trees. However, I also made sure to take sidewalks, so my steps couldn't be easily traced.

It wouldn't be right to say it was scary dragging the duffel across campus, avoiding security guards, diving into the bushes, etc. No, it wasn't scary. It was thrilling, and I could only hope there were no security cameras watching me.

After some extensive walking on concrete, I dropped the duffel and opened it. I took off Josh's shoes and put them on (with three layers of socks on, they fit better than my own), then put mine in the bag. If the police were to detail Josh's footsteps this night, they'd start here.

At long last I arrived at my destination: Molson Tower.

Now I needed a little luck. I found it. There was a Dumpster in the corner where Molson Tower and Science Hall met. It was perfect.

First I took care of the bottles. Opening the Dumpster, I took each bottle out of the duffel and placed it ever so perfectly inside with my gloved hands. I left the Dumpster open.

Then it was to Molson Tower itself. I wedged Josh's credit card in the door. After some frantic fidgeting, it finally popped open. Phew!

Again, believe what you will, but I schlepped that stupid bag up however many flights of old, creaky stairs. No one saw. No one heard.

It was no longer night, but not yet morning. I ducked under the bell and dragged the duffel bag into the dewy air. The knots in my stomach churned. I was so close.

I brought the duffel bag to the ledge and opened it. Peering down, I located the Dumpster. Now this had to be so perfect it was disgusting. I slumped Josh on the ledge. I was never much of a basketball player, but here I went.

Recycle this, Canada. I pushed him over. He sailed through the air and . . . *CRASH!* The Dumpster lid slammed shut from the impact. I couldn't have planned it better.

Acting hastily, I opened Josh's laptop and impatiently waited for the password screen. My shaking fingers typed in "Galaxy8" and after like an eternity I was in. The only problem was I couldn't find Internet Explorer. I wanted to scream. Calm down, Jenny, I thought, you're not going to get anywhere with this anxiety. I clicked on random icons, growing more and more restless. Then I clicked on something called Safari and the Internet window just popped up!

Josh was already logged into his Facebook page. I left the following note (entitled "Time to Die"): "I love the view from up here. Such a fitting place to die. School sucks. The world sucks. Macs rule."

Okay, I erased the last part but left the computer open on the ledge. It was time to get the hell out of there, but I had to exit one step at a time, literally. With my socks I wiped each stair clean of the duffel bag trail left in the dust. When I reached the bottom, I took off my third layer of socks and tossed them into the duffel.

Rushing back to the Dumpster, I threw in Josh's shoes but didn't put my own back on. Instead I gripped the nearly empty duffel bag and ran home in my two layers of socks.

It was five thirty in the morning when I entered Hippie Hall. I could smell eggs and hear someone in the kitchen. It must have been a weirdo, 'cause there was no chance a hippie was awake yet. Quietly, so incredibly quietly, I crept upstairs.

My room was cold and foreign to me. I wasn't sure if the smell of death was in the air or if it was just the bong water. Regardless, my room was a different place now, a place of violence and terror. But to the stoner eye it looked the same, and hopefully Jacinda wouldn't notice anything besides her missing bong.

In the mirror I saw bruises forming on my forehead and ear from when Josh had punched me, but they weren't that bad, nothing a little foundation wouldn't take care of. The bruise on my stomach was the worst, but obviously the easiest to conceal. As for pain—I felt none.

It all caught up to me then. Supergirl flaked and Jenny Green returned with all her typical Jewish anxiety. But I was too tired to deal with it. I was too tired to deal with anything. My nerves were completely fried.

So I hid the duffel in my closet, prayed that I wouldn't get caught, then fell onto my bed and into a deep, dark sleep.

PART TWO

Revenge of the JAPs

Chapter NINE

Prof Stone, looking cute as ever in his silly jacket and leather pants, continued with his lecture. ". . . and after Dostoyevsky was released from prison, he was a different man. It was perhaps his experiences behind bars that provided the material for his later work. . . ."

The class was taking forever. It was like the clock had stopped moving. It's not that I didn't like what Prof Stone was saying, I just wasn't in the mood for it today. I tapped my pencil, adjusted my watch . . . I was bored.

I started picking at my nails. It was such a dirty habit, I know, plus they were just growing back again, so . . .

Okay, okay, okay! I know some of you are just dying to hear what happened with that whole murder thing. In all honesty, the death of Josh Beck was still always on my mind. It'd only been a week.

Let's see. Okay, we'll start with the crime itself, although it wasn't really a crime, it was an act of self-defense. But I turned it into a crime by not reporting it because I'm an idiot, so for the sake of convenience we'll call it a crime. I like the sound of that better: the scene of my crime. Anyway, obviously I got away with it. Otherwise why would I be in class, eh?

Here are the CliffsNotes for a newspaper article about the "suicide" of Josh Beck:

STUDENT AT MOLSON KILLS SELF IN WORLD-WEARY HAZE

Police are keeping quiet on the details, saying only that he jumped from Molson Tower and died instantly upon impact.

His body, however, was found at the dump.

He posted his suicide note on Facebook.com.

While some students at the service were completely shocked by the sudden death of their peer, others said they saw it coming.

"Josh was always depressed. He talked about killing himself all the time," says sophomore Mitchell Myers.

Mitchell Myers wasn't the only one who'd said that. Apparently Josh was suicidal, and I was damn lucky.

So Josh "jumped" last Friday and landed in the Dumpster atop a big pile of unrecycled glass. The garbage is collected on Monday evening. Well, nobody must've read Josh's suicide post over the weekend or figured out where he'd jumped from or whatever, because nobody found him in time.

Off to the dump he went. A day later the police found the laptop at Molson Tower. So off to the dump *they* went.

By the time the police found Josh they were so fed up with the searching and the smell of the filth that they didn't even question whether or not it was more than a suicide. It was an open-and-shut case as far as they knew.

Wow. Talk about a major relief. Still, that's not to say I didn't worry. The days following the incident found me in a state of total nervosa (vocab I learned from Prof Stone, in case you're thinking it's not a word). I'd get into these yoga poses and not move at all for hours, except to bite my nails. All ten of my fingernails were practically nothing but cuticle by this point.

Chloe thought I hated her because of how little I spoke or moved. And I was sure the cops were going to be at my door any second. Or nab me in the street. Every time I saw a cop car drive by I instinctively froze like they'd think I was a tree or something. PS, I found a garbage can in the city where I discarded the duffel bag, my socks, shoes, gloves, hats, all of it.

I hardly ate, except of course for the on-campus TCBY. *Lots* of TCBY. If you were to excavate my stomach at the time you'd find nothing but fingernails and frozen yogurt. My loss of appetite kind of worked out, though, 'cause anyone who saw me thought I was totally in mourning. Obviously I had to play it like I was surprised and upset that Josh died. Oh, and I got this cool punch card, which meant every sixth yogurt was totally free. So if it was Monday I'd have a free fix by Saturday, and that's only when I ate once a day. See? Things weren't so bad after all.

I got a second piercing in each ear. I shopped more than Daddy's credit card could handle. I joined a kickboxing class but stopped working out otherwise. Can you believe I did all this in seven days?

Oh, and I put ash blond highlights in my hair. For some reason I tended to change my hair color whenever a guy didn't work out, and Josh was no exception.

Did I feel guilty? One day I did, although I wasn't sure guilt was the word. I felt like tampered goods. I was in a total funk about who I was and who I'd become.

It wasn't Josh's death that made me feel guilty. I mean, thanks to me there was one less rapist in the world. I pictured a parallel dimension where I hadn't killed Josh Beck, and that dimension seemed totally unfair. In that world I probably would've pressed rape charges and gone to court. My parents would be there crying and wondering if I'd ever be the same. The cute attorneys wouldn't ask me out because I'd seem like gross to them after what happened. And of course the Becks would hire some fancy lawyer and Josh would probably get three to five years with time off for good behavior to check e-mails, do some downloading, and whatnot. Then there would've been added tax dollars, the smear on Molson's record, and, knowing my parents, I would've been stuck going to therapy.

The way I saw it I'd done humanity a favor by saving all that time and money. No, it wasn't guilt I felt, more like confusion, bewilderment, estrangement, restlessness, paranoia, anxiety . . . ummm, the list can go on, but I'll stop there.

Jacinda's bong was another story. I mean, Jacinda and I didn't have the greatest rapport, so I was super nervous about telling her I'd broken her lifelong companion. I was crying and everything when I apologized to her.

Well, she was totally cool about it, so much so that we talked for ten whole minutes about Josh and life and everything. Who knew that killing Josh with a bong would end up bringing Jacinda and me closer together? I planned on buying the new one the first week of October, when Daddy's check came.

The futon was a different story. I felt so bad that she was sleeping on all of that dried blood. But I looked all over town and couldn't find the same one as hers. I thought of calling the company on the tag, but then there'd be shipping to deal with and no way to control when the futon arrived, and it would be a total scene. I just couldn't deal with it. Not to mention how faded and disgusting it was anyway. How was I going to match that?

Well, for the time being no one noticed the underside, and there was no smell or anything. I tried not to think about it too much, although it was kind of creepy sharing a room with the last remnants of my murderous deed.

Oh, and Raven's dog Orion was totally fine, not sick or anything. I guess a life spent eating hippie leftovers and inhaling armpit hairs gave him an invincible immune system.

Tomorrow was Yom Kippur, the Jewish holiday of fasting and repentance and the most important holiday of the year. It would be my day to wipe my bloody hands clean (in case the OCD hand-washing habit I'd developed didn't do that already). I'd even go to synagogue and fast all day as a symbol of repentance.

I was a sinner. I was a murderer. It was a knowledge I carried with me wherever I went. Like sex with Josh, it was rooted in my soul and defined me, even if I denied it.

However, I refused to let it destroy me. After I repented, I knew I'd be ready to eat and date again. But no sex, not unless the guy was really, really right this time. I wasn't going to be like abstinent or anything, just selective.

Class was still going on. All that catching up and the clock had barely moved. There was no way everything I just explained only took five minutes. Move it along, Prof Stone!

I planned on visiting my fave prof in his office later today. I needed to get in some face time—it was the first step toward getting an A. Besides, I had more sex and death secrets than Duftoyefsky or whatever his name was.

"To kill," Prof Stone declared, "is an act with many shapes, forms, intentions, and ends. In a world that constantly crushes our protagonist, can he rise above mere humanity by taking a life and showing that he's able to control reality or even change it? Perhaps not, for when he discovers he's just a poor, lonely, and moral subject, he's crushed by something much more powerful than the world outside his door: the unrelenting guilt in his vacant soul."

Don't you hate it when it's like the whole world knows your problems and is somehow throwing them in your face? Oh well, at least now I had something to talk to Stone about.

Chapter TEN

STARVATION, REPENTANCE,
AND FINALLY I START DATING AGAIN

So, so hungry. Sometimes I really hate Yom Kippur.

"Jenny, you're being all quiet again." Chloe's voice rang in my ears. She'd agreed to come to synagogue with me. It was this really nice one off campus, and I made her pretend she was Jewish because I didn't know the rules in Montreal. To play along, she also fasted. FYI, I discovered the Jewish holiday excuse was a round-trip ticket off campus for a whole day. How soon was Passover?

Anyway, I didn't respond to Chloe just now because for a brief moment a door swung open and revealed all the goodies for breaking the fast after services. I saw bagels. There was probably lox somewhere too. I actually don't like lox; I'm like the one Jewish girl who doesn't. Whipped cream cheese, on the other hand, was totally up my alley. I'd add a slice of tomato if possible too. The dairy wouldn't even hurt my stomach, since it was the first thing I would actually eat all day.

Ohmigod, I like never ate bagels anymore. I was so excited! Oh, wait. I'd forgotten I'd promised myself I'd fast an extra two hours after sundown to show God that I was repenting extra this year. Did you know TCBY is kosher?

I wasn't sure if I'd last those extra two hours. I mean, would it really make me that much more repentant? Probably not. The truth was, much of the fear and anxiety had left me by now. My old self was back with her energy restored. I will admit, though, that while the aftershock had settled, something still felt a little mixed-up inside.

So I was changed, but not enough that it would hinder my feast. This was the day and the time that my inborn Jewish appetite should finally return. Along with it I found new hungers, like the hunger for a buffet of whitefish salad and heaping mounds of kugel, the hunger for the touch of a man to make me feel protected, the hunger for that carnal pleasure of which I'd barely caught a glimpse. Great, now you probably think I was like ready for sex again. No, I wasn't gonna have sex just yet, but in the meantime my body yearned for that familiar make-out session.

I scanned the lobby, looking for candidates, but I was too preoccupied with the bagels to really get my search on.

"Jenny!"

"What, Chloe?" I whispered harshly. "Keep it down." We were getting looks.

Blushing, Chloe said quietly, "Why aren't you talking to me? What did I do?"

I could see she was nearly in tears, and it made me feel really bad. "Chloe, you didn't do anything."

"You've been like this all week."

"It's been a rough week."

"But you didn't even like Josh—" Chloe cupped her mouth. "I am so sorry I just said that. I have to go to the washroom."

I knew she was running off to cry, but I was too hungry and tired to do anything about it. So I let her go and didn't follow.

By the way, I went to see Prof Stone after that lecture. He was totally into me. He remembered my name and everything. I really played into his charms by laughing at his odd jokes and even touching his arm at one point.

We talked about whether it was okay to kill someone, and he explained how humans have done it before and will again, often for a good cause. Just look at Moses. He killed an Egyptian for beating a slave. And here we were celebrating what Moses did. It really put things into perspective. Yeah, Prof Stone was cool, and for a geezer he was pretty hot.

By the time Chloe returned, her mascara was all over her cheeks, so we decided to skip services and walk around. Hadn't she ever heard of waterproof mascara? I hated services anyway. I mean, they could be *sooooooo* boring. Maybe if I spoke Hebrew or something, or if like Prof Stone was the rabbi.

Chloe still wanted to break fast, as did I (okay, obviously I wouldn't last the extra two hours), so we waited in the Hebrew school area of the synagogue and just stared at the Hebrew letters on the bulletin board. Finally we heard the doors open in the sanctuary and the sound of hungry people moving toward the auditorium.

The feast was laid before us. I smacked my lips together. Hopefully, there wouldn't be too much ruckus; a hungry Jew could be pretty demanding. Everyone kept cool, though. Okay, so there were a few gabby women in their forties who complained about the food ("What, no sesame?") and some old man whined when anyone took more than two bagels, but that kind of stuff probably happens in church, too, right?

Chloe was next to me talking to this cute guy who looked a little too Jewish for her, as in like curly-sideburns Jewish. I thought the ones with the curly sideburns had their own temple.

Whatever. Food. I smelled hummus and toasted pita bread. Yes! They were so making the plate! But as I reached for the remaining pita a big hand snatched it up.

"You snooze you lose, yo." I was ready for war, but he put the pita on my plate and added a scoop of hummus. "Kidding. There ya go, sweetie."

The first thing I noticed was his eyebrows—professionally trimmed. His skin was naturally olive in tone, and I could spot the faux hawk creeping out from under his designer yarmulke. Now, normally it's not a good sign when someone's pants are sagging in temple, but somehow he made it work. Even the faux hawk was quickly growing on me.

We drifted off to the side, although I wasn't aware of moving. That was how he operated.

"Where you from?" he asked.

"Long Island."

"Word. I love you New York girls. Represent. You know how to party, though. We'll get to that. Damn yo, you got the whole package. How old are you?"

"Eighteen," I lied. It was like this mischievous impulse just kicked into gear.

"Lucky girl. Imagine how you'll look at twenty-one. Hey, I'm the one to know around here. Dizzy D."

Wait a second. What did he just say? I need to rewind that: *".D yzziD .ereh dnuora wonk ot eno eht m'I, yeH .eno-ytnewt ta kool ll'uoy woh enigamI .lrig ykcuL"*

"Lucky girl. Imagine how you'll look at twenty-one. Hey, I'm the one to know around here. Dizzy D."

He *did* say Dizzy D. Was that like a name?

"Cool," I said. "I'm Jenizzy G. Or Jenny Green. Whatever you prefer."

"Jenny. Definitely. I'm surprised you ain't heard of me yet. You ask anyone in any temple or club who Dizzy D is and they'll say they know me. You got a car?"

"Not yet."

"We'll check out my Audi later."

I didn't want to sound too easy, so I said, "Maybe some other time."

"Definitely some other time, girl. That's what I've been talking about. We ain't gonna get our freak on right now!"

He was pretty smooth, and by the time he left, Dizzy D had my phone number and a tentative promise that I'd meet him again. He disappeared from the lobby as if I was the only reason he'd come. I made a mental note to change my Facebook and MySpace info as soon as I got home so that it matched my new age.

Well, I knew where his name came from—I suddenly felt dizzy. Or maybe I just hadn't eaten enough, so I ate his leftovers.

I looked around for Chloe. Somehow she was still talking to that same guy. I had no idea how far they'd gotten into Exodus, but I could tell from her facial expressions that she wanted out. So I ran over to her and said I had an emergency and then dragged her to the bathroom.

The coast was clear. I washed my hands for like the twenti-eth time that day, then Chloe and I stood before the mirror and atoned for our sins. She went first. "Okay, I'm really sorry I made that comment earlier about Josh. And I promise to be a better friend in the months to come. Ummm . . . oh yeah, and I'm sorry I've been drinking so much but, you know, it's high school! I think that's it. Oh wait, I'm sorry I stole some of your eyeliner when you weren't home."

"It's okay, Chloe."

"Now I'm done. Your turn."

"Okay, I'm sorry . . ." I thought about the obvious thing. But was I sorry? I just wanted to move on. The truth was, he deserved it. I was a lot of things, but sorry wasn't one of them. "I'm sorry I've been too quiet and moody these past few days. And I'm sorry I always choose the dumbest guys. And I'll try not to shop as much anymore and spend Daddy's hard-earned money on things I don't need."

"Jenny, you don't choose the dumbest guys. It was one guy."

Chloe had forgotten all the stories I'd told her about my freshman and sophomore years. How every guy left me feeling stupid and hollow. Sure, I had great times, but it was like every guy was a different book with the same ending.

Oh well. If you don't succeed, try again. Isn't that how it goes? The world was full of possibilities.

Chapter ELEVEN

AND NOW FOR A SHORT BREAK
WHILE I BUY JACINDA A NEW BONG

"Hi, I'm here to buy a bong."

"Okay. What are you looking for?"

"You know. It's like that thing with the hole at the top and you like smoke marijuana out of it."

"Right, I know what a bong is. But what specifically are you looking for? One-footer? Six-footer?"

"Six footer! Jeez, that's taller than I am. No, I don't know, do you have like one and a half?"

"How does this look? Glass changes color, and there's Papa Smurf's head at the base. Smoke gets trapped in his eyes. It looks really cool."

"How much?"

"One eighty."

"Ohmigod! I had no idea bongs were so expensive. It's just glass."

"I'll throw in the sister piece and a pouch for free."

"Sister piece?"

"The slide. It's where you put the chronic."

"Chronic what?"

"The marijuana. Are you a cop or something?"

"How about one twenty?"

"Come on."

"What else do you have?"

"A bunch of new bubblers just arrived. You wanna check those out?"

"Bubblers?"

"It's like a bong/bowl hybrid. You fill the bottom with water."

"How much?"

"A hundred."

"Sister piece included?"

"Bubbler doesn't have a sister piece, but I'll throw in a pouch for free and a one-hitter, too."

"Wait. I'm here for a bong. What's your cheapest?"

"This one here. It's a plastic one-footer. Thirty bucks."

"No, I want the pretty glass ones."

"This one's a hundred fifteen."

"Sister piece?"

"You got it, sister. And see all the pretty colors?"

"Ninety bucks."

"A hundred."

"Pouch and hitter included."

"Sure. And it's *one*-hitter."

"What, do you use it once and then throw it out or something?"

"Not even close."

"A hundred bucks with tax included, free sister, free pouch, free one-hitter."

"Deal."

Sucker.

Chapter TWELVE

DIZZY DATING

Dizzy called later that week and we made plans for Friday. He talked about a three-course meal and a drive in his Audi, and I didn't want to miss a thing.

In my eager mind I pictured late-night dancing, drinking with college kids, and maybe some heated make-out sessions. Obviously that meant I needed to be off campus for more than two hours.

The first thing I did was visit Dean Sanders and request special permission, but he did like a total 180 on me. "Jenny, that was a one-time thing to help a student in distress. I wouldn't be in this position if I just handed out free passes to Montreal." What a creep!

"So how do I obtain special permission?"

"With an absolutely valid excuse, which I now know you don't have. So if we see you leaving this school, we're going to be paying extra-close attention."

Great, that was like the total opposite of what I wanted. So I went to the next best person.

"Edgar!"

"Shhh, Greenie!" Edgar whispered.

"No talking!" the nerdy teacher yelled. Oops, that's right, we were taking a quiz. Well, that wasn't going to stop me. I resorted to good old fashioned note passing.

Me: I need to sneak off campus tonight.

Edgar: Leave me alone!

Me: Edgar, please! I need your help.

Edgar: You're a pain in the ass, Greenie. Meet me after class behind the theatre.

Me: I love you, Edgar! So . . . what'd you get for problems 10–14?

Then after class I met with Edgar, whose eyes were darting every which way like a neurotic spy. He confided, "What you're seeking exists, but I want something in return."

"Come on, Edgar!"

"Okay, okay. They call it Ditch Molson. You follow the brown ribbons to the far northwest wall. There's a hole that goes under."

"How do you know this?"

"A kid I was tutoring told me about it. I used to see an older woman and I had to sneak out to meet her."

Older woman? Who, your grandma? He was so cute, though. And helpful. He told me everything I needed to know. Score!

Dealing with Raven was no problem. She was like the coolest Housemother in history. I simply told her I had special permission to leave campus for a while and she just, like, believed me. Amazing.

I neatly folded my dress clothes into my messenger bag and, wearing sweats and a T-shirt, went off to find my escape route. My adventure started at the soccer field, which was right by the woods.

Following Edgar's instructions, I searched for an elusive brown ribbon and found it tied to a tree branch like ten feet above my head. It brought me deeper into the woods. With the camouflaged brown ribbons as my guide, I traversed a terrain known only to the brave students of Molson's past.

As I ventured, I wondered, was Dizzy D worth the trouble? The truth was, it didn't matter. There was a thrill in my gut that made me think I'd be doing this for no reason at all. With my recently dark past, there came a new rebellious present. Okay, there was also a part of me that said, why are you always getting yourself into these situations?

Ditch Molson was well concealed by the dirt, which I hastily cleared away. Soon exposed was a slim wooden board. I moved it aside to uncover a ditch leading under the wall. C'est cool. After a deep breath, I took the plunge.

On the other end it was the same: another wooden board covered in dirt. I pushed *that* aside and came up in like this totally empty park. Okay, while I was in the ditch it felt kind of like a coffin. It gave me both the chills *and* the thrills.

Anyway, like a bandit I covered my escape route so that others might one day traverse the ditch. Now where was the nearest sink?

One thing I gave Dizzy D credit for: The man had class.

He picked me up on the corner of St. Laurent in his silver Audi A8, and I just stood outside the car for a minute. I mean, it was so beautiful, like it belonged to royalty. Of course I'm not sure royalty would be pumping hardcore rap, but hey, it's the twenty-first century, so maybe they would.

Waiting in the car, Dizzy smoked a cigarette and wore the coolest designer clothes. He sat there looking at himself in the mirror, hardly acknowledging my presence. Yet for some reason he attracted me; he was so . . . vain.

"Jenny Green. You getting in or what?"

"Nice wheels."

"I know, I own them, and everything I own is nice. I got a hooked-up Jeep Wrangler, too. You know, for some old-school flavor."

I swear like half the people walking by said hello to Dizzy. It was like I was with George Clooney or something. I could've back-flipped into that beautiful car.

"What? You don't want me to know where you live?" Dizzy prodded.

"Not yet," I said mysteriously.

"Whatever."

Off we went.

The interview process began.

"So how old are you?" I asked.

"Wait just a sec, baby." He was getting a call. "*Salut* . . . yeah . . . St. Denis. Yeah, I know it. Gelateria . . . yeah. Nine o'clock, eh. *À bientôt.*" He hung up and explained, "I had a friend track down the name of this ice-cream parlor for us. The thing is, the place we're going for dinner, their desserts are all fancy and shit, but I like making it special. And I thought to myself, Jenny's a simple girl, a nice old-fashioned cone of ice cream would bring back memories. Sound good?"

"Works for me. As long as they have frozen yogurt."

"Would I take you to a place that didn't serve fro-yo?"

"Anyway, are you in school?"

"Uni? Hell no. Waste of time."

"What do you do then?"

"I invest. I trade. I dance. You look so good tonight I could eat you up, girl."

"You smell really nice. What is that?"

"You got that Jewish nose power, huh? Issey Miyake, accept no substitutes."

"You think my nose is big?"

"Calm down, baby. It was a joke. You got some good sense to you is what I'm saying."

Meanwhile, I'm not kidding, Dizzy waved to like half the cars that passed by. Every minute or so there'd be some random guy honking and throwing nods in Dizzy's direction.

He informed me, "I was born and raised here. I got this town on lock. Anything you need, literally anything, I can get for you. I'm the King of Montreal."

Yannis was a glamorous spot tucked away in the heart of Westmount. It was small and quiet, with live piano music. It glowed. And to describe the food as tasty was to describe Dizzy's car as a piece of junk. I tried to avoid looking at prices, but obviously I checked them out, and there weren't any! Do you know what that means?

Dizzy asked, "How's the wine?"

"It's only like the best I've ever tasted." And the glass was so gorgeous. Thank God the waiter didn't ID me. I guess in the right dress I look much older. "*Sooo* good."

"That's 'cause it's a Castello Banfi Brunello. 1985. From a single vineyard in Tuscany: Poggio dell'Oro. Means "golden hill" in Italian. You can't ask for a better bottle. Let it breathe. Swish it in your mouth. It don't come cheap, baby. How 'bout the salmon?"

"Like you need to ask."

"You're right, I don't. I'm glad you're enjoying it, Jenny. A girl like you deserves the best. Hey, I'll be right back."

God, it was like the fourth time he'd gone to the bathroom.

The first was to take a call, but for the other three he didn't give a reason. Was his bladder malfunctioning or something? Oh well. I had this killer salmon and wine to enjoy, with or without him. I was so impressed with Dizzy D's knowledge of the hottest places to do anything. I guess when you're rich, that's life in a nutshell.

Dizzy D returned and had like this huge sneezing attack right there at the table. He almost knocked over the precious bottle of wine, but I saved it. He approved of my quick preservation instincts. "Nice moves, girl," he told me. "I can't wait to get you on the dance floor."

"Dizzy dances," I teased.

"I move to the groove and flow like snow, yo. You got rhythm too, eh? You know what that means: You like to get it on."

"What?"

"You're a girl with a past."

"Uh, no. Not me. I'm still a virgin." PS, I decided to tell people I was still a virgin. I mean, would you count that night with Josh?

"Virgin, eh? Not for long you're not."

Gross. Still, I wondered what it'd be like to make love to Dizzy D. He was so confident about everything. But there was something vulgar about him too. Maybe it was all that music he was playing where they said "bitch" and "ho" at every turn. I just pictured Dizzy only being capable of loud, raunchy sex and never making love. If I was more experienced, then maybe that would've been appealing, but there wasn't a chance in hell I was losing my reborn virginity to some hip-hop homeboy.

Dizzy D paid for the bill without looking at it, using an

American Express black card. Whoa. That's like the coolest credit card in the world. I heard somewhere that it's got no limit, and I even touched one once—it's like smooth charcoal or something. He saw that I was transfixed by this little card and joked, "Don't leave home without it."

The gelateria was a big lie. They didn't have frozen yogurt. I was pretty irritated about it too, because I'd totally prepared myself for a small cup of nonfat vanilla with almonds or pistachios. Dizzy assured me, "Don't worry, we'll go somewhere else. This must not be the place I remembered."

Yet he wasn't moving. He just kept peering into the ice-cream case and then looking at the entrance. It was bugging me how Dizzy was obviously here to meet someone, so I blurted out, "Why'd you lie to me? I heard you on the phone, Dizzy. You're being all shady."

"Jenny, I swear I thought this place had fro-yo! You're right, though, I'm waiting on this stupid friend of mine. He left a bunch of stereo equipment in my car. Here he is."

Dizzy's friend was much older than I expected. And when I say older I mean like forty or something. Yuck, the guy kind of looked like a rat. His hair was super greasy, and he had one of those slimy mustaches pasted under his big nose. He and Dizzy exchanged handshakes, then spoke only in French so I didn't understand a word. Chloe was supposed to teach me one of these days.

After like five minutes of French, Dizzy turned to me. "All right baby girl, you sure you don't want nothin'?"

And at that moment the worst feeling came over me: I kinda wanted to kill him. "Dizzy . . ."

"Okay, okay. Let me give my man back all his audio equipment and then I'll take you somewhere special."

Then Dizzy opened his wallet and handed me a Canadian twenty. "Here. This is your ice-cream money. You think about what you wanna get and I'll be right back."

So I stayed in the stupid nofrozenyogurteria and glared at the old lady on the crisp bill. I wanted to kill her, too. She was lame-looking.

I did something pretty weird then. I took a small pencil off the counter and poked out her paper eyes. What the heck was wrong with me?

Finally Dizzy strolled back in and gently took me by the arm.

"All right, princess, what'd you decide?"

"TCBY?"

"TCBY it is."

And like that the bad feelings were gone.

After dessert, Dizzy decided I was sober enough to drive the Audi. Legal enough was another issue, since I didn't have my license, but trust me, you wouldn't have been able to resist either.

I couldn't decide what was smoother: Dizzy or his car. It was like it drove itself. It just cruised, you know? Each acceleration, every brake felt like somehow this massive vehicle was customizing itself to my body. I could've driven all night in that thing. I drove up and down the Ville-Marie Highway, even out to the casino, and finally, when it was time to call it a night, I pulled up to my corner.

"Jenny Green. You been smiling all night."

"Yeah."

"Mon petit chou-fleur."

Instead of explaining what that meant, he leaned in for a pretty intense make-out session. I'll admit, it was a little uncomfortable because his gangster rap music was playing, and every time it said something mean about women I felt like Dizzy was thinking that way about me, but other than that he was a pretty great kisser who used a bit too much tongue.

And talk about busy hands. He couldn't keep them off me. He was tame about it, though, not what I expected. Sure, his hands moved fast, but when they arrived at somewhere we both liked he took his time. It was our first date, and I totally should've stopped him after a few minutes, but it felt so good to be touched that we went on longer than that.

Eventually we came up for air, and he shot me a smug look that both attracted and disgusted me. I mean, he was really a little too into himself. Whatever, I hopped out of the car and waited for him to vanish into the night.

PS, to his credit I later found out that what Dizzy had said to me earlier in French was a "term of endearment" and totally romantic! Something about a little cauliflower . . . on second thought, maybe I needed a better translation.

Chapter THIRTEEN

DIZZY DOUBLE-DATING
WITH A SHOCKING TWIST

It didn't take too long to realize that Dizzy D was not the man for me. For starters, our relationship was illegal, no matter what country we were in, and he was also kind of a big jerk. Plus, how many trips out to that dank, dirty ditch could I take?

So it was over between us. I just hadn't told him yet. I mean, he took me to Style Xchange and let me buy whatever two items I wanted. Diesel sweater, Juicy jeans. Would you give that up right away? I would've been a fool to turn away that offer, and I made up a jingle to commemorate "My Favorite Things":

Juicy Couture sweat suits, sweatpants, and sweatshirts.
Triple Five Soul and Miss Sixty short skirts,
Small Diesel sweaters made for Jenny Green,
Sevens are some of my favorite jeans!

Okay, okay. So it's a little shallow to be leading a guy on just so he'll take you to fancy dinners and buy you expensive clothes. This I knew. But in my defense, I was sixteen years old at the time, plus it's not like I totally despised him.

I got what I wanted from the relationship and he got what he wanted. Sort of. I say sort of because I'd been kinda prude with him. We'd been dating for like two weeks and my clothes weren't any closer to hitting the floor. Not even my top.

In all honesty, things with the Dizz seemed too good to be true. He was very good to me, but he really wasn't very romantic about any of it. It was like he was going through the motions. How many other girls had already been here, given the task of choosing any two wardrobe pieces they wanted? And come on: Dizzy D? I couldn't even bring him home to my parents.

When I talked to Chloe, we both agreed that it was time to bail. I'd return the clothes if need be. I'd throw up all the food Dizzy had paid for. Hopefully, he'd just be upset and wouldn't ask for any of that back.

The only thing was, Dizzy had this superhot friend Stefan, and I thought we should totally hook Chloe up. That meant a double date, so I had to postpone the breakup until after that. We didn't really have a breakup plan, but thank God my best friend would be there in case anything went wrong.

Watching Chloe dig her way through Ditch Molson was a

story in itself. Let me just summarize with the image of her butt in the air and two words: "I'm stuck!"

How someone skinnier than me could be stuck I'll never know, but that's for another time. Needless to say, we made it to St. Laurent intact.

Dizzy drove, saying Stefan would meet us there. It was Chloe's first time in the Audi, and she was loving it. I could tell within minutes that she understood why it was so hard for me to let Dizzy go. She didn't even mind the blaring rap music, normally my biggest complaint. In fact, she was familiar with it, singing along at times. I'll admit it was pretty funny watching Chloe spew lyrics about killing white people and having sex with prostitutes.

It was on the way to dinner that I felt a headache coming on. *Great timing,* I thought, and I was totally out of Tylenol. I wondered if I'd caught Dizzy's cold (he *was* always sniffling), or perhaps all the loud music had finally given me a tumor. I prayed it wasn't a migraine.

"Hey, can we stop at a dep or something?" Dep was short for *dépanneur,* which is like a drugstore. I used the local lingo as often as possible. Chloe was teaching me French in her spare time. Anyway, no one heard me because of the blaring music. "I said, can we stop at a dep!" It just made it worse.

Dizzy stroked my neck and lowered the volume. "What's wrong, baby?"

"I have a killer headache."

"Here."

Dizzy popped open his glove compartment, and with his fast hands removed a bottle before I could see it. I heard the pills rattling, and when he offered two of them I didn't even ask; I swallowed them both. Hopefully, I'd feel better before we got to the restaurant. I didn't want some stupid headache ruining my night with Chloe.

Dinner was at a killer restaurant called Buena Notte. Real Italian food. George Clooney ate there whenever he was in town. As we pulled up, my headache wasn't only gone, but in its place was this almost euphoric feeling. It was totally weird, but maybe I was just excited to be out with Chloe again. My body was like tingling! Really strange, but I'd been known to have weird reactions to aspirin in the past.

By the time our entrées arrived, I could tell it definitely was not just excitement. Everything was slow moving and viscous, like oil and water. It was a major mistake to sit on the right-hand side of the table, too, because every time I raised my left arm it bumped into Dizzy's right one. I guess I was kind of all over the place. Somehow I was totally carefree about it, though, more and more so with each new glass of wine.

Chloe and Stefan were kind of hitting it off. It was clear he was into her, but she kept quiet mostly. We'd heard Stefan was a major, major player, so maybe that's why Chloe was keeping her distance. Or maybe it was because she knew that by this time tomorrow Dizzy would be hizzy (short for history). Of course, it could have been the whole age thing.

Stepping out on a caloric limb, I ordered the gnocchi. I wish I could say how tasty it was, but for some reason I was beyond drunk by the time it arrived. After two bites that tasted like mush, I felt my stomach oozing.

"Dizzy—I'm dizzy."

"Stop drinking so much wine."

"Jenny, what's wrong?" Chloe interjected.

"I'm okay. I'll be right back. Keep busy, Dizzy."

"You're hilarious tonight, girl. Hurry up before your food gets cold, eh."

After convincing Chloe to stay, I staggered to the bathroom and blindly found the toilet. I guess you can figure out what came next: *blllleeeeecccch!* I told you I was wasted. In retrospect, I should've ordered the salad.

I'll skip all the nasty details, but I should mention that while slumped against the porcelain I thought of Josh. He deserved what came to him. I ran to the sink to wash my hands like twenty times.

I'd never had such a low tolerance! My first thought was I must be losing weight. I popped two sticks of sugarfree gum while giving myself a baffled look in the mirror. Was I like pregnant or something? The doctor had said no, but maybe it doesn't show up early on. Or I totally had an STD! Those can take a while to show up as well. Damn you, Josh Beck!

So I know it sounds like I was freaking out, but then I actually started laughing. I couldn't remember being this wasted in my whole life.

I staggered back to the table.

"Jenny, are you okay?"

Ignoring her concern, I asked back, "How's your dinner, Chloe?"

"*Sooo* good. You wanna try some?"

"No thanks, babe. What do you think of Stefan?" I probably should have saved that question for when the guys weren't around.

Chloe stuttered, "Uhhhh . . . he's really cool."

"You're really cool too," Stefan said. "Whaddaya say after dinner we grab a drink somewhere?"

"I think Jenny's had enough to drink."

Dizzy butted in. "I'll take care of Jenny. Don't worry, Chloe, she'll be home by midnight."

"Well, I don't know. . . ."

"Jenny, are you gonna ruin your friend's good night?" Dizzy asked.

"Jenny hasn't ruined anything," Stefan said. Obviously, someone was trying to score points with Chloe. "Maybe some other time."

Dizzy put his arm around me. "Jenny and me, we're gonna chill for a bit. Drive around, maybe. We'll catch up with you."

Chloe glared in my direction. "Jenny, is that what you want?

Are you sick or something? We should get back to—" Don't say it, Chloe!

Now here I did something really stupid. "No, of course I'm not sick, don't worry about me. You two go dancing. It'll be fun." Okay, I'll admit it, I also wanted to ride around in the Audi one more time before kissing it good-bye.

Dinner ended and, reassured like a hundred times over, Chloe went off with Stefan for drinks. I got into the passenger seat of Dizzy's Audi, and he drove us around the city, then headed to his apartment.

I guess I'd kinda forgotten my original plan, and as we pulled into his garage I suddenly wondered what the heck I was doing there. It would be harder than I thought to put an end to things now. Where was Chloe when I needed her?

Of course Dizzy's apartment was hooked up like everything else he owned. Aside from the gigantic high-def television and killer stereo, he even had all this pointless nice stuff like a foot massager and a Buddha statue. It would be the perfect apartment if only I lived there and not him.

The liquor was slowly wearing off. When I came to my senses, we were on the couch watching a gangster movie. It was only a matter of time before Dizzy put the moves on, and at first I responded, but then remembered I had a plan. I pulled away from him abruptly.

"Damn, Jenny!"

"Dizzy, we have to talk."

"No, that's exactly what we *don't* have to do. No more talking."

"We're through, Dizzy."

"What do you mean, we're through?"

"It's over between us," I said defiantly. I was so proud of myself.

Dizzy made this impatient grunting noise, and like a little kid he stood and paced around the room. "Damn, Jenny, you don't even know me."

"What do you mean, I don't know you?"

"You didn't even give it enough time to see my affectionate side."

"Dizzy—"

"I'm serious, Jenny! I'm not who you think I am. I like to read poetry and shit. I go apple picking."

"Apple picking?"

"See! That's what I'm saying. I wanted to show you the side that no one sees. I wanted you to see Danny."

"Who's Danny?"

"My birth name. Daniel Davis. He's the man *behind* the machine."

"The *machine*? Look. Who are we both kidding? It doesn't matter. Danny. Dizzy D. Whoever he is! He wasn't meant to be with Jenny Green."

"Fuck!" he exclaimed. Then he went on this bitter tirade in French. I had no idea what was being said, but there was no mention of cauliflowers. I guess maybe I deserved it.

"What are you saying, Dizzy?"

"Little princess gets whatever she wants: clothes, dinner, money even. I take her to the nicest places and let her drive my car. And she says nothing. Tonight she says nothing. It's only once that little credit slip is signed that Jenny Green states her mind. Right? Right!"

It was true. I'd been using him like he was a personal ATM and not giving it much regard. Maybe I did owe him a little more. I wasn't caving, though. "Dizzy, can I just go home?"

"No."

"What do you mean, no?"

"We're talking about this, Jenny. You been using me. I want something back."

"Want something back?"

"I treated you nice because I really liked you. I still like you. I wasn't messing around. I liked talking to you. I liked kissing you. That's why I bought you those things. Not because I thought you'd go away if I didn't, but because I genuinely wanted to make you happy. Don't you genuinely want to make *me* happy?"

I could tell this was gonna be one of those nights where everything goes in circles. I thought of calling a cab but knew somehow Dizzy would keep me there.

The truth was, for all his ramblings we both knew he wanted one thing. I thought about it. He was good-looking. I didn't feel threatened. It wasn't like with Josh or anything. And there was the guilt, too. If it would end things once and for all, I guess I kinda figured why not.

"Well, what do you want, Dizzy?"

"I don't know."

Here it came. "You want like a blow job or something?"

Now, for you girls who've never done this, that is, give a guy a blow job just to shut him up, I commend you. For everyone else (and there are more of you than you'll admit), well, sometimes a sacrifice must be made. Besides, it was just a blow job. It's not *that* big a deal.

Dizzy definitely liked the idea. "Yeah, Jenny. Yeah, that's what I want. You'll love it, baby. I keep it nice and clean just like every-thing else."

Sure, Dizzy, sure. Then afterward we could read poetry and shit. Reluctantly I droned, "Fine."

"To the bedroom!"

So we proceeded to the bedroom, where Dizzy unzipped his pants. I felt queasy, but fortunately the wine was still kicking in my blood.

The bitter time was at hand. I headed down there for you know what. Dizzy was the happiest I'd ever seen him. "I love this shit," he said. "Wait just a sec, though. I wanna get something."

"What?"

"My lucky hat."

"A hat? No."

"What do you care?"

"Fine, Dizzy, get your hat."

His pants were at his knees, so he hopped over to the closet, where he looked for his stupid hat. I hated that he gave me more time to think about what I was doing, but he was back in position shortly, wearing his "lucky hat" (I forget what kind of hat it was, but it wasn't Yankees) backward on his head. He nodded as if approving commencement. "All right. Let's do this."

So I commenced. I'm gonna spare you the details, but let's just say it was taking a while. During most of it, Dizzy said stuff like, "I love this shit" and "oh baby, you don't know how good this feels" and blah blah blah while rubbing my hair and whatever. Gross.

Anyway, like I said it was taking forever, so I asked impatiently, "Don't you want to finish?"

"Not yet, baby, not yet. Keep going. Ooohhh, yeah." Gross gross gross! I really don't like talking about this. The worst was yet to come, though.

Dizzy made some weird, disgusting noises. It sounded like the moment had arrived, but I was dead wrong. "Wait, Jenny, wait."

"What? Are you done?" I asked eagerly.

"No, not yet. . . . What about — ———?" I'm sorry, but I've censored what he said because it was so heinous.

"What's — ———?"

"You know, where you —— —— ——— — — —."

"What? I don't know how to do that."

"Just use your thumb."

I held out my thumb in disbelief. My innocent thumb. Around it was Bubbie's ring. She'd given it to me for graduation, and it was originally a normal ring, but her fingers were like huge so I used it as a thumb ring. It was precious to me.

"Dizzy—"

"Please! If you just did it, it'd be over with already."

You know what, I'm just gonna skip ahead. All you need to know is that I was still kind of wasted and just wanted to get everything over with, so yes, I complied with his utterly disgusting request.

I ———— — —— — — —. He ————— —— - ———— ——. I imagine by this point some of you with more experience have figured it out. All I can say is . . . yeah. Gross.

Fast-forward. The job was done. I raced to the bathroom and rinsed my thumb and hand over and over again. It was no use. My pretty little fingers were forever tainted. I was too innocent for this.

By the time I left the bathroom, Dizzy was dressed in a robe and sitting in a chair, holding his keys. "You're the best, Jenny Green."

I didn't want him to drive me home. I didn't want to see him again for the rest of my life. So I stormed from the apartment before he could stop me.

When I hit the sidewalk I was already in tears. Not ready to go back to Molson, I walked endlessly. No matter how hard I tried, the tears wouldn't stop falling. I even stopped once to vomit. Why did I agree to such a disgusting task? I should've been stronger. I should've bailed when the true pervert came out. This totally wasn't worth the cost of dinner!

It was a good half hour before I realized the worst part: My ring was missing. Bubbie's ring! If it were any other ring I wouldn't have cared, but this one possessed like more sentimental value than any other jewelry I owned.

It couldn't be. It just couldn't be! In my head I pictured all the possible scenarios. It must have slipped off in the sink when I was super-soaping my dirty little fingers. That made sense. Right?

A million more images popped into my head. I even pretended I hadn't seen it just before the plunge and could've lost it ages ago. I pictured losing it in bed or in class. I pictured myself getting really bored and playing with it while watching television. I pictured it on my dresser. The closet. The roof. Prof Stone's lecture. Oh anywhere, anywhere but that one place, that dark nether region from which no thumb has returned unscathed. Anywhere but there!

Life totally sucked that night!

I stopped in my tracks and turned back toward Westmount. Was I really going back? Did I even want the ring now? I did. I couldn't lose that ring. But I could always wait and have a friend pick it up or ask Stefan, maybe. No, if tonight was the night from hell, there was no point in stretching it out to another day. With my head down and my thumb ringless, I schlepped back to Dizzy's apartment.

It took like twenty minutes. The doorman recognized me, so

he just let me in. I reached Dizzy's floor and marched to his apartment. The door was open, so I entered without knocking.

There was laughter coming from inside—four or five guys speaking French in his den.

I approached cautiously. They still didn't notice me as I peeked in from behind a corner. What was all the laughter about? I wondered.

Well, I found out when I saw the most horrific thing I'd ever seen in my life. It was worse than bad hair on a date with George Clooney. It was more terrifying than Josh's dead body on Jacinda's technicolor futon. It was a video of everything that had just happened only an hour before. Everything. There must have been a camera in the closet—the same closet from which Dizzy had retrieved his "lucky hat."

Now, I know I said I was an actress, but this was far from how I'd imagined my television debut. It was totally appalling.

I turned away in disgust. One of Dizzy's friends was in hysterics. *"Dizzy, qui est cette prostituée?"*

"She's no one, yo. Just another trick."

"Tabernac!"

Dizzy kept going: "One of those high-class Jewish girls. Daddy's probably a lawyer. He'll sue my ass if I put her on the Web. She ain't even legal anyway." He *knew*? *"Merde*, the best part is coming."

As they prepared for the finale, I stumbled out the door and ran as fast as I could to get away from that wretched apartment.

What I'd seen in there was totally unfit for a princess. It was so traumatizing I didn't know where to begin.

In a flurry I hailed a cab and headed home. I cried like three gallons of tears into the backseat.

No one close could ever know what happened. Not even Chloe.

She was in the den when I entered Hippie Hall. It was pretty obvious how much I'd been crying. She rushed to my side. "Jenny, what happened? Oh, are you okay? Come here." She gave me the biggest, warmest hug in history. "Is everything okay?"

"It's over, Chloe."

"Oh, my precious Jenny. He was such a scumbag. He didn't deserve someone sweet like you. I love you so, so much. And I have to tell you something. Stefan made me promise not to."

"I don't wanna know."

"Jenny, Dizzy D is like the biggest drug dealer in Montreal. And he's a total cokehead. You can't ever see him again."

"I won't, Chloe." It made sense to me. I was so naive I wanted to kill myself.

"That's not all, Jenny. Tonight, when you asked for aspirin, Dizzy gave you some sort of painkiller. Perk something."

I couldn't even speak.

Chloe was crying for me. "Remember we said we'd only date guys we both approved of? I don't approve of Dizzy D. He's a total jerk."

No wonder I'd ordered the gnocchi. No wonder I'd done all that nasty stuff at Dizzy's apartment! The world was spinning once more, like earlier tonight, like early September. How could someone be so corrupt? I cried in Chloe's arms and went through like a hundred tissues.

Then later I stumbled into the bathroom and found the volcanic soap for emergencies only. I washed my hands again and again and again. Then my mouth. Then I showered. Then I vomited one last time. *Oy vey,* I thought, and I never ever think that.

When I finally got into bed, it was like four in the morning. Jacinda was fast asleep, and her boyfriend wasn't with her. I swear it hadn't been there before, but I could smell the blood from beneath her futon. It smelled fresh and inviting.

Suddenly I was infuriated. Who did that . . . that . . . that fucking pervert think he was, taking advantage of me like that? Did he think he was special because he dealt drugs? Did he think I was just another girl from one of those rap songs? Well, I wasn't. There were things about me that you didn't know, Dizzy. Hidden things. Deadly things.

I almost tore Herman's arm off, I was gripping my bear so hard. There was no cap to my anger, it just grew and grew. Dizzy D had something coming to him, and his friends wouldn't think it was very funny, yo.

It was at this moment that I realized how different a person I'd become. Inside me that secret knowledge I'd been suppressing resurfaced, and Jenny Green sank deep, deep down into the muck. Supergirl was called to duty, and she'd been taking her multivitamins.

Before falling asleep, I told myself one thing and one thing only: Dizzy D would be Dizzy *dead* by this time next week.

Chapter FOURTEEN

ROTTEN APPLES

Planning a murder took an unprecedented amount of concentration. And I thought yoga was challenging.

I talked little and ate less. Every waking hour was dedicated to visualizing the act in my head over and over again. I thought of every possible scenario, because I wanted it to be perfect. I couldn't kill Dizzy D in Montreal because like *everyone* recognized him. It needed to be someplace far away.

Then there was the weapon. Obviously I couldn't get a gun. Knife, then? Poison, maybe?

The day after the whole incident I went back to his place to retrieve Bubbie's ring. I brought two weirdos as a security measure.

Dizzy said he found it on the mattress, but I knew where he'd found it. As he gave it to me, I did my best not to inhale. The whole time I tried not to look at the sleazeball, but he kept nagging me and pinching my butt. He was lucky I didn't take a wrench to his skull.

There wasn't a single moment where I didn't want to like spew vomit all over the apartment. Anyway, I made it pretty clear that we weren't speaking again, but he still called later that day and left a message.

His voice reminded me of the awful things he'd put me through: the video, the drugs, the missing ring! It's like it deserved its own *E! True Hollywood Story.* And I could tell he was calling just to spite me, for his own mental masturbation.

I set October 14 as the final date because there was supposed to be this huge thunderstorm the next day. It would wash away whatever trail I'd leave. Perfect. October 14. Sunday. The day God wakes well rested and gets back to work (the Jewish God, that is).

I awoke as Supergirl. Her mission was to rid the earth of male scum in the name of women everywhere. FYI, Supergirl showered with some of the finest skin and hair care products on the market, Aveda and Kérastase. Supergirl was ready.

Of course, she still had a bunch of stuff nagging her, like the fact that the police would most definitely come around after the murder. There was no way they wouldn't. She considered breaking and entering to steal the video, but it would compromise everything.

Then there was the alibi. Where was Jenny Green on Sunday while Supergirl was killing Dizzy D? Jenny Green was at the campus library, then the cafeteria.

So I went to the library that morning, making sure to tell at least two hippies (then I realized that two hippies might still not remember, so I told Chloe, too). I found the cutest librarian there and made him help me find all these pointless books. I totally flirted with him to ensure he'd remember me. He followed me upstairs to the little study nooks. "God, I'm gonna be here all day," I told him.

I pretended to study for an hour, then left under the radar. As for the cafeteria plan—it was pretty F-ing brilliant. Earlier in the week I pretended to misplace my swipe card (it's like a campus credit card) and borrowed Chloe's, telling her I'd let her use mine once it was found. Surprise, surprise, my swipe card popped up on Saturday night! I gave it to her and in a very roundabout way made sure she'd use it on Sunday in the late afternoon.

You might be thinking about security cameras, but for the most part they didn't exist. Not in the library, not in the cafeteria. Aren't Canadians so trusting?

Back to the murder. I didn't want Dizzy to call me that day because it would leave a trace, so I Ditched Molson and found this out-of-sight pay phone in Montreal. There was no turning back . . . unless he didn't answer.

"Yo."

"Hey there."

"Jenny!"

"My name's not Jenny."

"Whatever you say, girl. Now, what the fuck, not-Jenny? I'm not good enough for you anymore?"

"You're good enough, Dizzy. Too good. I miss you." Gross. But how else could I make sure he'd be game?

"I miss you, too, sweetie pie. I wanna hang out. I'll do anything you want."

"How about apple picking?"

"Apple picking?"

"Remember, Mr. Sensitivity?"

"Ohhh, yeah. Of course, Jenny. It's just that it's getting cold out. I don't know if there'll be any apples left."

"So we'll go to see. There's an orchard in Sainte-Anne-de-Bellevue."

"That's like an hour away in Île-Perrot."

"Just forget it, then."

"All right, all right. . . ."

"I'm already on my way out of town. Meet me in St-Anne by the dock on the water." He agreed foolishly. I prayed he wouldn't tell anyone where he was going.

With little time to act, I raced to the nearest bus stop and took the first bus out of town. It dropped me off exactly where I needed to be, and I walked a block over to the dock. Nobody would recognize Dizzy D or his flashy car out here.

Sure enough he showed up, albeit ten minutes late and in his Wrangler. I was a little annoyed because I kind of wanted to drive the Audi again, but I guess it worked out for the better, since the Wrangler was fairly inconspicuous in this part of town.

As he pulled up, I put on my second cheapest gloves and hat (only one hat this time). On my feet were men's shoes that were two sizes too big. I was already wearing my sunglasses—not my Versace ones, though, since they could draw attention or get ruined in the scuffle.

I got into the passenger seat. I carried a taser and a switch-blade in my purse. Yes, a switchblade. Okay, it's not the smartest weapon of choice, but Supergirl had the energy to murder with her bare hands.

The taser's actually a revenge story. Last year in social stud-ies, Richard Farber threw a slice of pizza at me when no one was looking. So embarrassing. I told you it was a crappy year. So later I stole a taser from his book bag. What it was doing there I'll never know, and go figure it would finally come in handy for something like this.

Dizzy was his old stupid self. "Damn, Jenny, you look as good as when I last saw you. Even with that silly hat. It ain't that cold yet, shit. Have you lost weight? Where's the love, girl?"

"What love? Let me see your phone."

Dizzy handed it over without complaint, and I checked for outgoing and incoming calls. I was the last one for incoming and the last outgoing was before that. Phew.

Dizzy fussed, "Hey, what the hell you doin'?" I turned off the power. "What the fuck, girl!" He snatched it back.

I told him, "Turn it on and I'm turned off. I'm sick of you always talking on that thing. Can we go now?" He kept it off.

"You gotta tell me the way. I ain't got GPS in this car, and it's been a while since I've been apple picking." *A while* as in *never*, I was sure.

Supergirl navigated Dizzy farther and farther away from Montreal. Everything that was Jenny Green remained at the dock. Supergirl's destination was near.

There was no one for miles, and the orchard was closed. Dizzy was right about the apples being out of season, but it was what Supergirl had been counting on. Total isolation. Nothing but her, Dizzy, and the rotten apples.

They walked beneath the autumn trees. The late-afternoon sun filtered through the branches. It was cold out, but not so cold that she could see her breath or anything. "Just cold enough," she said.

Dizzy observed, "Damn, girl, you're all weird today! And you kinda look like a man with that hat covering all your hair. It's all good, though. Come here."

He drew her near. Not a chance. She pushed him away and ran through the orchard to tease him, shouting, "If you can catch me, you can have me."

That really got him moving, but the adrenaline was on Supergirl's side. She wandered farther into the orchard, to the Yellow Delicious apples. Quickly she climbed a tree and hid. In her beige

BCBG brushed velour sweatshirt she blended in with the dead leaves and apples.

Soon Dizzy advanced. She could see him picking a few good apples that were left and chucking them for no reason. What a waste. Soon he would be nothing but waste himself.

Before long he was below her, sneaking through the trees. Supergirl waited for the right moment . . . it was near. It was now. She pounced down on him and smashed her arms over his head. He collapsed to the ground, but she wasn't finished with him. She grabbed the taser and zapped him before he could even open his mouth for help.

He was squirming like a fish out of water. Forgoing the switch-blade, she grabbed the biggest apple she could find, a half-brown Yellow Delicious, and forced his mouth open with her thumbs (the thumb, Dizzy, she remembered to use the thumb).

The apple fit snugly in his throat—Supergirl made sure by slamming it in way past his bloody teeth with her foot. No air could pass through at all. She shoved and shoved until juicy bits of apple were splattering onto his face. Dizzy could do nothing but take it. Soon his legs stopped kicking. Silence.

He was Danny now. That's what his obituary would say (well, it would probably say Daniel). Supergirl stood over her work and stared endlessly at his still body. As she reapplied lip balm, she felt nothing but satisfaction.

Grabbing a nearby apple, she took a bite. That apple was the sweetest she'd ever tasted.

Relying on the same hidden strength I'd used with Josh, I cleaned off Dizzy's face and schlepped his body all the way back to the Wrangler. I took his keys out of his pocket, where I found a small bag of cocaine.

I drove away, heading toward Montreal. Night was falling. About twenty minutes into the drive I came upon the perfect stretch of nowhere. Nothing but woods and dry grass. The road was completely deserted. First I needed to take care of the body, so I parked the Jeep in the woods and dragged it to a spot I found worthy as a dumping ground. I ran back to the Jeep, trying as often as possible to step on fallen branches so as not to leave footprints in the dirt.

I drove another ten minutes until I felt I'd gone far enough. Again I headed into the woods. Taking the bag of cocaine, I dumped it on the passenger seat and floor of the Jeep. I didn't want it outside, because the rain could wash it away. If everything worked well, it would look like a botched drug deal. I abandoned the Wrangler.

I walked two miles to a bus stop and soon enough the bus arrived. I boarded and made eye contact with no one (which was easy with my sunglasses on). Sitting in the back, I looked out the window the entire time. My faint reflection glared back at me. But my face was hidden beneath a snow hat and behind sunglasses. It was a stranger looking back at me.

Around eight that night, I got back to Hippie Hall. I'd already disposed of my gloves and hat, and then my shoes. I now wore the sandals I'd planted by a Dumpster earlier that morning next to some books, which I grabbed as well.

When I walked through the door, Chloe was hanging out with Raven in the den. They asked where I'd been, and I said the library. Chloe handed me back my swipe card, and I casually asked what she'd bought with it. One of those premade Asian salads. Got it.

I told them I'd be done in a sec and headed to my room, where I changed. After washing up, I joined them but I was still absent. All my words were lies. Every laugh was carefully planned. I played it so cool that they didn't notice the change, not even Chloe.

This time it was for real. There was no accident. No self-defense. I'd murdered Danny, and every girl in Montreal was better off for it.

Chapter FIFTEEN

AND THE OSCAR FOR BEST ACTRESS IN A HOMICIDE GOES TO . . .

The day after Dizzy's murder was like the longest day ever. Supergirl totally vanished on me. Hard truth hit like a brick. It churned over and over again in my head . . . I was a murderer. For real this time. It was scary.

I spent like half the day in the bathroom and the other half in bed with Herman. There was no way I was going anywhere, not even Prof Stone's lecture. And by the way, it wasn't raining. When was it gonna rain? They said it was gonna rain!

I freaked and broke out in random sweats that were totally gonna give me acne. Even when I put a bag of ice to my forehead, they wouldn't stop! I was itchy, too. Convinced I'd developed a nasty rash, I applied some emergency antifungal cream to every spot where the itching arose. Before the day was through, I'd covered practically every part of my body. I was like a poster child for zinc oxide.

Even Jacinda expressed concern. Unfortunately, it was one of those days where she was around more than usual. Taking traditional rips from her awesome new bong, she kept offering some to me because she said I looked totally stressed out. "Jenny, it's just pot. It's not like, heroin or coke."

Ugh. Don't talk to me about cocaine. All I said was, "Jacinda, please."

"You're just really stressed, hon. I mean, you're practically green, Jenny. Green Jenny. Jenny Green. Ha!"

I wished she would just shut up. I didn't know how much more I could take.

Every time I closed my eyes I saw blood. I wanted to paint a canvas all red or knock myself over the head just to get it off my brain, but I was too afraid to move, let alone paint or hurt my precious head. I decided that since I'd be changing my hair color, I'd make it auburn, which had red in it. For now I just chewed my nails, though, until they were crescent stubs. When was it gonna rain?

Finally, around six in the evening, the sweet pellets of rain fell to the earth as promised. The storm swept through and eventually covered the whole region. Some of the hippies lit candles in their rooms and watched through the window. I watched in the dark.

Chloe called from class just to make sure I was okay with the storm and everything. I was more than okay. In my imagination I watched as the footprints and tire tracks dissolved into mud and water, destroying clues and illuminating oh so many false leads. The sound of harsh rain against the window was my only source of comfort that day.

I realized that my fear of getting caught was once again the core of my agony. It wasn't guilt. Never did any doubt enter my mind that what I'd done wasn't the right thing to do. Much later on the doubts would arise, but not then.

The day before had been magic. It was superhuman. I was the judge and jury. I was the executioner. Dizzy couldn't hurt anyone anymore.

The rain cleared, and day two after the murder was spent awaiting the phone call. I was sure the police were going to get me; if not as a suspect, then as an acquaintance of the infamous Dizzy D. They'd find the videos. They'd hear about our dinners and shopping sprees. They'd call.

My cell phone rang. Wow, that was quick. Not even noon yet. This was not a good sign. They'd found his body. They were onto me.

It was a number I didn't recognize. I almost didn't answer but wondered, would it somehow seem suspicious?

My hand was quivering as it reached for the phone. "Hello?"

"Ohmigawd, Jenny?"

"Yeah?"

"Jenny, what's up?"

"Who's this?"

"Are you like serious right now? Ohmigawd she doesn't recognize my voice."

"Stacia?"

"Uh, yeah. Like your best friend from high school Stacia. I got a new phone. I haven't talked to you in like a month. Did you get my e-mail?"

"I guess not, but I'm on my way to class."

"Oh, bummer. Well, listen real quick, because we'll have plenty of time to catch up . . . when I visit in three weeks!"

"Shut up."

"It was in the e-mail. I'm coming with Julie, Lolo, and Veronica. The Juicy Couture warehouse sale is in two weeks. Did you forget?"

Wow, I'd totally forgotten. Every year, for one day only, Juicy has this crazy sale in the middle of nowhere in Quebec. It's like the Mecca for JAPs everywhere, and they flock from as far as Long Island to buy enough clothes to fashionably dress a Third World country, leaving only a trail of Splenda packets and bran muffin crumbs behind. We'd gone with our parents last year, and it was pretty incredible. I guess it was time again, but I didn't wanna think about it.

Quickly I agreed, and only afterward did I realize I'd just granted permission for Veronica Cohen (the same JAP who stole my prom date) to sleep under my roof. Whatever. Maybe I'd kill her, too. Kidding!

In my head I saw flashing sirens and felt the handcuffs choking my wrists. My body grew cold as a jail cell. They'd call.

My ringtone blared. Private number.

I answered. "Hello?"

"Hey."

"Chloe." She was calling from Stefan's landline, I guessed—it never showed up.

"Stefan's wondering if you've seen Dizzy D." Chloe and Stefan had started seeing each other, by the way. I thought it was a bad idea, but Chloe swore up and down that Stefan and Dizzy were two totally different people. Stefan didn't even like Dizzy that much.

"Why would I have seen Dizzy D?" I asked a little too meanly.

"I don't know! I'm just asking."

"Well, I haven't."

"Okay. Good-bye."

She hung up in anger. I felt bad but would have to deal with it later.

Half an hour passed, during which I itched a little, chewed my nails, changed locations on my bed, and squeezed the crap out of Herman. It was already two in the afternoon and I hadn't eaten a thing. My sole source of nutrition was the jumbo bottle of Evian I kept bedside. I finished it, then gnawed on the cap and peeled the label. Time passed.

Then, at seven . . . another private number. Jenny Green, meet your doom.

"Hello?"

"Hi, I'm calling from Sprint. How would you like to save a hundred dollars over the next year?"

"Ohmigod, will you shut up! If you call me again I will hunt you down and murder you!"

"Murder. That's what these other companies get away with—"

I threw my phone against the wall and it nearly broke. I was losing it.

There came a slight knock on the bedroom door. From the other side: "Jenny." She sounded both timid and indifferent, meaning it must have been one of the weirdos. "Jenny, there's two cops here to see you."

After all that waiting, they showed up at the door. Of course. Holy F, they were at the door! I looked like crap! I had a matter of seconds to switch from borderline nut job to confused ex-girlfriend.

"I'll be down in a sec!"

Okay Jenny, okay, pep talk. Remember all those plays you were in? Remember all that time you spent auditioning in front of the mirror? This'll be a piece of cake. Think of it as an audition for *Law & Order* or one of those shows.

I scurried to the bathroom and cleaned myself up. I hadn't realized it but I'd been crying, and my face was totally bloated. But I didn't have time, so a rush rinse and makeup job was the best I could do. Then I totally screwed up on the eyeliner, so I just rubbed bronzer all over my face.

Giving up, I trotted downstairs.

One of the cops was old and scary-looking with like this huge mustache, the other was young and cute (although I'd find out later he was kind of a pervert). Now, how does a girl who has no idea why the cops are at her door act? "Uh, hi. What can I do for you guys?"

The younger cop smiled sincerely. He replied with a thick Canadian accent. "Hello there, Jenny. Soory to bother you. We're here in regards to a friend of yours."

I pretended to be confused. "Ohmigod. Chloe. Is Chloe okay?"

"Chloe?" the older one said gruffly. "This has nothing to do with anyone named Chloe."

"Thank God. You looked so serious, I thought maybe she was hurt or something." I didn't like the older one. He was a real prick. Officer Prick.

The young one put his hand on my shoulder. "Can we sit down somewhere? Somewhere private, eh?"

So I brought them to my room. As an extra security measure I let them take my bed, and I plopped down on the futon. Inches beneath me was a giant stain of evidence; I'd be lying if I said it didn't totally give me the jitters.

The young one introduced himself as Jim. The older one didn't introduce himself. I wondered, was this good cop/bad cop?

"Do you guys want something to drink or some Hershey's Miniatures?"

But they weren't interested in my hospitality. Officer Jim began the interrogation. "The reason we're here, Jenny, is in regards to a guy named Daniel Davis."

"Dizzy D?"

"Right. He's missing, Jenny," explained Jim. "He's been missing for over twenty-four hours now. Any ideas aboot where he could be?"

"None. Dizzy and I stopped seeing each other like over a week ago. Oh, crap. Should I not have said that . . . because, you know, I'm like a minor?"

"The age thing we'll save for another time," Officer Prick said gruffly.

"How come you stopped seeing each other?" Jim asked.

"Because he was totally shady. At first I thought he was like this sweet guy because he took me to all these fancy dinners, but then I started wondering where the money came from. Oops. I probably shouldn't be saying that to the police either."

Officer Jimbo chuckled. "It's okay, Jenny. We've been looking into Dan for quite some time, eh." Officer Prick shot him a look that said, *You're talking too much.*

Now it was Officer Prick's turn. "After you and Dan broke up, did you communicate?"

"He called a lot. I never answered or saw him again."

God, there it was. If one single person knew I'd gone to the orchard with Dizzy, my entire cover was blown. Nervous sweat trickled down my face. The older cop didn't flinch, and Jim was just kinda checking me out.

It was Jim's turn again. "Did Dan have any enemies?"

"He wouldn't tell me that kind of thing."

Officer Prick interrupted. "Where were you this Sunday?"

"Sunday? God. Sunday. The library. The cafeteria. Here. I hung out with Chloe that night. Mostly the library, though. Got some papers due."

"Can someone else attest to that?" Officer Prick asked.

"Attest?" This guy was scaring me.

Jim cut in, "When was the last time you saw Dan, eh?"

"The last time I saw him was last Wednesday, I think. We went on a double date with Stefan and Chloe the night before, and I left my ring at his apartment. I went back the next day to retrieve it, and . . . well, let's just say I didn't want to see him after that."

"How come, eh?" Officer Prick wanted to know. I knew they'd eventually see the video, if they hadn't already. It made me a victim, though, not a killer.

"It's kinda personal," I said.

Jim assured me, "That's fine for now. One day, however, we might need to follow up on that. That's okay?"

"Yeah. I mean, you guys are cops, you can do whatever you want, right?"

"Now Jenny, ya have your rights," Jim said sweetly. "I guess we're aboot done for now. If he calls, you'll let us know?"

"One last thing," Officer Prick butted in. "You said you were in the caf. Did you use one of those campus credit cards?"

The "caf" was his word for cafeteria. I pretended to think

about his question. "Ummm . . . yes. Yes, I did. And yes, if Dizzy—I mean, Danny—calls I'll obviously let you know."

They both gave me their contact info and then later, as they were leaving, Jim lingered in the doorway. "Hey, can I ask you a really big favor?" he said.

"Yeah. Anything," I replied eagerly.

"I have a brother. Tim. He's a student here at Molson. Anyway, he's been having a tough time making friends, ya know, and I was wondering maybe . . . maybe you could, ya know, have lunch with him?"

It was an odd request, but anything to please my investigating officer! "Sure, Jim."

"Great. How aboot I'll have him call you?"

Wow, if there was one sign that you weren't a suspect, this was it. And it worked out perfectly, because I could use Tim to keep tabs on Dizzy's case. I was totally a femme fatale, but obviously I wasn't gonna kill Jim or Tim or anything.

Unless, of course, they did something to deserve it.

Chapter SIXTEEN

A TRAGIC DAY FOR STONERS EVERYWHERE

I knocked quietly at the open door. "Guess who's back? And this time I brought cookies."

Prof Stone was at his desk, buried in work. You should've seen the way his eyes lit up at my entrance.

"You're too kind. Tell me, have you been enjoying *Women in Love*?"

"Excuse me?"

"The book we're reading."

Is that what we were reading? Never heard of it. I hoped there was a DVD I could rent. "Oh, yeah. Hell yeah. So much Eros."

"Yes, plenty of that. D. H. Lawrence always injected his novels with lots of Eros and Thanatos."

"But I wanted to talk about Thanatos today."

"Right. The death drive. Hitler. Supermen. The power to die. The power to kill."

"The power to kill," I repeated. "I mean, how could Hitler

do those things? Not just to Jews, to whole countries?"

"He's not the first. Every race has blood on its hands. But Jenny, your fascination with death intrigues me. Don't be afraid to embrace it. Many famous minds have said that we all have a killer inside us."

They found the body of Daniel Davis that Wednesday. It was major, major news. It graced every newspaper headline, not just in Montreal, but across Canada. The newspaper wasn't too specific (and there was no mention of apples), but it hinted at a botched drug deal. *Shocker!*

Police were scrambling for clues and leads. Was it a gang? Was it the Mafia? Little did they know their murderer was a sixteen-year-old ex-girlfriend in designer jeans.

There was a general sense of mourning and bewilderment in Montreal after the news broke. I mean, Dizzy grew up there and knew everyone. Plus, he supplied half the world with drugs, so like, how was everyone gonna get high?

I know I should've been even more worried now that they'd found the body, but instead I'd reached this state of numbness. It was like my upcoming date with Tim (or whatever it was called) made everything okay. I was gonna get away with it.

That same night Jacinda was out, so Chloe and I had a sleepover (yes, I took the futon). I apologized for snapping over the phone and convinced her I was okay with Dizzy's death.

"I love your body," Chloe said randomly.

"Wanna trade?"

"Totally."

"Chloe, are you serious? You're like totally beautiful."

"You really think so? God, sometimes I just wish there were no men in the world. We should just be lovers."

We got a laugh out of that. It felt good. I was young and innocent again that night. For a second, I even forgot I was inches away from Josh Beck's dried blood.

Oh man, I hoped everything would work out. I didn't want to go to jail. I didn't deserve dry oatmeal and stale biscuits for breakfast, or a cellmate named Bertha who tied her pigtails with cable cords. I deserved the Juicy warehouse sale and Fire-Roasted Veggie Salads with grilled chicken, hold the cheese. Wait, if you were arrested for murder as a minor, did they automatically let you out when you turned eighteen?

Probably not. *God, please don't let me get caught!* I prayed to myself. I prayed for normalcy.

The TV was on in my otherwise dark room. Muted footage of soldiers in Iraq filled the screen.

"Jenny, can we please never fight again?"

"Never again."

"And you're sure you're okay? Two deaths is a lot to handle."

"Two dead jerks, Chloe. Why should I be upset?"

"It's . . . scary. Is it just me or this the craziest year ever?"

It wasn't just her. And no matter how much power I held in the palm of my hand, as I watched the television shove chaos down our throats, I realized I was still completely helpless in a crazy world.

Chapter SEVENTEEN

BALLS OUT

It was Wednesday night, and I had a fake dinner date with Officer Jim's brother, Tim, at this little resto-bar called Le Pistol. Why we didn't meet on campus was beyond me, but he'd called the day before and insisted on Le Pistol. He said he'd be the guy in the Canadiens cap (as in the hockey team). If I was lucky he'd give me the 411 on Dizzy's case. PS, I left Molson officially—there was no way I was hanging with this guy for more than two hours.

Let's see . . . Canadiens cap, Canadiens cap. There he was! Wow, while my memory of Officer Jim was a little hazy by this point, Tim looked very similar. The main difference seemed to be the hat, the glasses, and the long sideburns. Plus he wore like the worst clothes: an oversize checked shirt and baggy jeans with all these strange zippers leading nowhere—it was like an older person's idea of what a teen would wear.

"Hi, Tim!"

"Hello," he muttered. He sounded totally nervous.

Taking a seat, I grabbed a menu. "So hungry. Actually, what am I doing? I already know what I want, presuming they have veggie salads!"

"That's cool, dude. Thanks for meeting me. My brother said so many nice things aboot you."

"That's so sweet of him. Well, I'm glad to help, Tim. And I'd be happy to set you up with some of my housemates . . . I mean, they're okay, I guess."

"Ya. About my brother, though. He's like the man."

"Oh yeah? So has he been talking about the case? You know, Daniel Davis?"

"Daniel Davis? Oh. No, he doesn't talk aboot that with me."

"Bummer. I just can't stop thinking about it. I hope they catch the killer."

"Oh, they will. Jim will. He's really smart, ya know. Like a genius, maybe."

Tim tended an itch on his massive sideburn, and I just couldn't stop staring. There was just something about him . . . oh my God. Not in a million years will you believe what I noticed right then. The sideburn was peeling! It was a fake! Tim was Jim!

Should I be nervous or flattered? I wondered quickly. Either Jim secretly wanted me, or he was doing an awful job spying on me. It had to be the first. Jim must have seen the video and gotten ideas; very, very poorly executed ideas.

Wanting to play it cool, I tried to glance away, but the jig was up. Tim, I mean Jim, was completely aware of what I saw, and his eyes went like crazy wide. In turn, I just kind of bugged out.

Considering this guy was a cop, I should've been more supportive, but I couldn't help it. He was weirder than this girl Sandy, who lived in Hippie Hall and painted her pet lizards, then hung them from the ceiling to dry. He was so weird I felt a slight urge to kill him, but of course that was wrong. He was just a feeble male, and if I had a dead body for every one of those I'd be in big trouble. So instead I bailed.

The city was a blur beside me as I ran back to campus. It seemed like I was making progress, but soon enough a firm hand gripped my arm. "Jenny, it's not what you think!" Jim exclaimed. "You can't run away from me. I'm a cop!"

And just the way he said that, like so balls-out, as if a badge gave him a license to be a pervert or an asshole, made me shudder with disgust. So I turned to face him and gave him a swift knee to the groin. "Then arrest me, *Tim*."

". . . . ."

Oops, I must have hit him a little too hard, because he was on the ground now and like struggling to breathe. Well, whatever, he shouldn't have tried to manipulate me like that. He was a total perv. An Officer Perv.

Okay, I totally just kneed Officer Perv in the balls. Nice one, Jenny. I was definitely gonna be a suspect after this. Great, just what I needed! And right when I had a big AP exam tomorrow.

Ohmigod, my AP exam!

After checking the campus directory, I discovered that Edgar lived in the Science Sector, a big house like Hippie Hall that provided shelter for all the future scientists of the world. Wow, and I thought math was Edgar's specialty. For a nerd, he was so cute!

Anyway, I could've called him, but I figured a house call might be more convincing. Besides, I didn't know where else to go and was sure like a barrage of police would be waiting for me at Hippie Hall.

Before knocking I straightened myself up and tried not to look like a girl who'd just de-sperminated a cop. What a creep Jim was! If he tried to arrest me for that I'd . . . I'd . . . I'd kill him! I thought of Dizzy—it was like a strange nightmare.

You should've seen the look on the face of the kid who answered the door. "Athletes' Quarters is two houses down."

"No, I'm here to see Edgar."

"Really?"

"Really. Is he home?"

"Right this way."

Walking through Science Sector, I expected like gizmos flying through the air and Legos and test tubes everywhere, but it was spacious and well furnished, just like the other houses.

I came to Edgar's room and knocked. From the other side of the door I heard his voice. "What's the password!"

"Edgar's a *huuuge* nerd who has a password for his room. Is that it?"

"Greenie?" The door eagerly swung open. It was good to feel loved.

Cut to ten minutes later. Edgar's still shaking his head. "I don't get it. If you suck so bad at math, then why are you in this class?"

"Edgar, will you help me or not?"

"I'll help you *cheat*, Greenie, but under one condition."

"What do you want, Eddie?"

"I want you to take me to a party. A good one. And you're not like my date or anything, but you have to hang around me for the night."

"Edgar, I barely party."

"That's fine. But when you *do* go to a party, I want you to take me."

"Deal."

And that was that. What followed was the most nerdy, elaborate plan I've ever taken part in. Edgar had a miniature walkie-talkie set. The speaker part was in Edgar's watch and the hearing part was in the clicky thing on a pen. During the test, Edgar would just whisper the answers into his watch, and I'd put the pen next to my ear to hear the answers.

"This set means a lot to me. It's from my friend in Hungary."

Whatever, Edgar. I'm sure your cyber pen pal won't find out. Gimme.

And that was how I passed my AP exam the next day. While

Edgar had this totally criminal look on his face during the exam, I felt like a total loser playing *Mission: Impossible* in AP Calc. But I got an A, which was totally cool. For a nerd, Edgar definitely had balls. PS, I still hadn't seen or heard from Officer Perv since the night before.

There were a bunch of exams throughout that whole week. I did pretty well in all of them except for this Canadian Studies class Molson required for all international students. Who knew "Eskimo" was a curse word in Canadian? I'm not joking. Who really says "Aboriginal," anyway? And did you know British Columbia wasn't in Great Britain or Columbia? Oh well, I could always buy an atlas before midterms.

Focusing on grades really helped me shed all these uncomfortable vibes, but I'd be lying if I said Dizzy D was yesterday's news. The ordeal was in my bones now. Like it or not, I was a killer. And in the most offhand moments I found myself relishing my past, waiting for a chance to kill again. Kind of twisted, I know, but I was eager to help rid the world of more human scum. It was like my part-time job in Montreal. No, no. It was my duty.

To celebrate not having to study (or cheat) for a while, Chloe and I "Ditched Molson" and hit up St. Laurent in the city. And no, I wasn't flaking on Edgar—I had plenty of time to hold up my side of the deal. Tonight was for my best friend and me. We found a bar that didn't ID and partied until dawn.

That night it snowed for the first time. Really, really snowed. I mean, there'd been frosty mornings in October, but this was a whole new level. You could hardly see, there was so much white in the air.

Chloe and I ran outside and did a dance with our mouths open, tasting the delicious flakes as they melted on our tongues. Chloe was so beautiful in the snow—she was the greatest friend I'd ever had. And dancing with her amidst the flurry of snowflakes made it so easy to totally forget I'd ever had those annoying friends back home in Long Island. My bitter reminder was just hours away.

Chapter EIGHTEEN

THE INVASION

I awoke the next day to what sounded like geese.

It was freezing in my room. For some odd reason the window was open a crack. Oh wait, I remembered now. I'd opened it at like five in the morning when I'd wanted to taste more snowflakes and let them engulf me with their numbing coldness (okay, obviously I was still dealing with things).

Reluctantly I got up to shut the window, and through the glass came the noise of relentless gab. Geese? I was confused until I heard a distinct voice on the street below, "Veronica, don't get snow on my suitcase, it's worth like a bunch of money. I can't believe we're here! Juicy sale! Holla!"

That was Stacia. The JAPs had arrived. It seemed there'd be two kinds of flakes swarming Montreal for the next few days.

I sneezed. I hoped I wasn't sick. Or maybe I wanted to be sick and that way I didn't have to deal with them. I threw on some

Molson mesh shorts, but at the last second changed into Juicy sweatpants. The last thing I needed was wardrobe critique.

"Coming!" I shouted so they'd stop incessantly ringing the doorbell. I practiced smiling. When the excitement felt genuine, I opened the door. "Girls!"

"Jenny!" Stacia yelled back. "What up, girl! Hugs. Kisses." We exchanged them. It was Stacia, Julie, Lolo, and ugh, Veronica Cohen.

Stacia and Julie had put on a few pounds, Lolo looked exactly the same right down to her Uggs and Lululemons, and Veronica was like enormous. Okay fine, I lied, Veronica was super skinny, but who even likes that these days?

"I can't believe how long it's been," I said as the girls amassed in the foyer. "It's so good to see you!"

Julie responded, "Ohmigawd, you have such a cool place. Is there heat, though?"

"Yeah, it's on. I'll turn it up, though. It takes a while."

"You have a computer, right?" asked Lolo. "My mom e-mailed me with all the clothes she wants me to pick up for her."

BURP! Veronica belched. It was pretty gross. Then she spoke, "Sorry. I ate like the nastiest sandwich in the car. Do you have a bathroom?"

"Down that hall, last door on the right."

Veronica took off. There was almost a moment without sound, but Stacia killed it. "Jenny, you look amazing. I'm so jealous! Hey, can you call a sister back or what? I've called you like a million times this week."

"You did? I guess my—"

"Ohmigawd, this is gonna be freakin' awesome!" Stacia shouted over me. "Juicy sale! Holla!"

"Hollaback!" chimed Lolo (who was already texting someone). I wasn't even sure if they knew what "holla" meant, let alone "hollaback." I sure as heck didn't.

"So how was the drive?" I asked.

Stacia answered while applying lip balm. "Gawd, we've been up since like five in the morning. The drive was pretty good, though. We only stopped like a hundred times for bathroom breaks. Right, Veronica?"

"F you!" Veronica yelled from the bathroom.

"So cool that Julie has her license now," continued Stacia. Julie just kind of smirked. Yeah, good thing Julie had her license and a car, otherwise she probably wouldn't have been invited. With me gone, Julie was easily the weakest link in the JAP clique. God, I was so thankful I didn't have to see these girls every day.

"Jenny, this is only half our luggage. Can you help with the rest?" Lolo asked. Half? Jeez. They brought enough luggage to build a house. Need I remind you, they were staying for three days. Not to mention that each of them brought an additional empty suitcase just for all the clothes from the Juicy sale. A little excessive, eh?

Not wanting to crowd the den, I suggested we take everything up to my room. It was a big mistake, though, 'cause once they put their stuff down, there was like nowhere to walk.

Looking around, Julie noticed the lack of space. "I really like your room, Jenny. It's quaint. But where are we gonna sleep?"

"Well, my roommate usually sleeps at her boyfriend's, so one of you can crash on her futon."

The girls gave the futon a once-over. It was obviously not up to their standards. "Maybe you want to sleep on the futon, Jenny," Lolo kindly suggested.

"No, Lolo, I don't. One of you can have it."

Stacia seized the opportunity, "That's me."

"What? Why?!" Julie snapped.

"Because I called it."

"Stacia, I was clearly hoping to sleep on a mattress or whatever. My eyes have been like basketballs lately."

"Julie, I called it. Besides, I'm better friends with Jenny. And I set this whole thing up."

"Stacia! I can't sleep on the floor. I drove! I have a bad back!"

"Then how about we share it?"

"You know I hate sharing beds, Stacia."

"Julie, are we really gonna do this?"

"Girls, shut up!" Lolo yelled. "If I can't have the bed, then *I* should get the futon. I didn't get shotgun on the ride here."

They were loud enough to wake the house. I could already hear doors opening as the hippies were snatched from their morning slumbers. This wouldn't be good.

Tears were swelling in Julie's eyes. "You know about my back, Stacia!"

Finally I offered a plan. "Julie, you're gonna have to share. You and Lolo can get the futon, me and Stacia can sleep on my bed."

"What about me?" Veronica cried. I'd intentionally excluded her. Remember that whole prom thing? I'll get to that in a sec, by the way.

I groaned. "You can nap on it in the afternoon." Hmm. She didn't like that. "How about this: I'll share my bed with Stacia and Lolo. Julie and Veronica get the futon."

They all agreed to it, more or less. Okay, now let me get to Veronica before I forget. I wasn't entirely hung up on getting revenge for what she did. *Buuuut*, if some circumstance arose where it seemed really convenient to make her life a little harder . . . well, let's just say I hated loose ends. Split ends too. God, my hair was like a disaster that morning, so I announced, "All right, I'm gonna take a shower."

"When can we shower?" asked Julie.

Lolo spurted, "Oh and Jenny, my mom talked to your mom, who said it was cool that I store a bunch of my stuff in your bathroom."

"Ohmigawd, wait." Stacia gripped my arm. "First, do you notice anything different about me?" She turned and profiled for me until it was blatantly obvious.

"Ohmigod, Stacia, you got a nose job."

"I wanted it to be a surprise. What do you think?"

"It's amazing." Amazingly moronic was more like it.

Crash! It came from down the hall. "What the hell are you doing?" That was Raven.

"I am so sorry," someone replied. Uh-oh, where was Lolo?

I rushed to the bathroom, where Lolo was setting up shop: hair dryer, curling iron, straightening iron, grooming products. One girl and the bathroom was already swamped. How'd she even get here so fast?

Something had been broken—on the floor were smushed wax and shards of glass. "Hi, Raven," I said.

"Jenny, is she a friend of yours?"

"Yeah, I have some friends in town for the next few days."

"She broke my incense candle. And left it there."

"I said I was sorry!" Lolo cried. "I was just trying to make room for the hair dryer."

Raven was pissed. Until now, I'd never seen her be anything but chill. "What are you, like, Vidal Sassoon?" she barked.

"Eww, two for one at CVS? I don't think so."

"Well, can you just be careful?"

"Look, don't be such a psycho, I'll buy you a new candle."

"I'm a psycho? Get out of my house, you fucking stereotype!"

Obliged to mediate, I stepped between them. "Raven, let me explain. These girls have been traveling all day. Lolo, you didn't mean that. This is my *housemother*, Raven."

After I shot her a telling glare, Lolo came to her senses. "I'm sorry," she said. "It's nice to meet you. I didn't mean to break your candle. I feel terrible. I'll buy you a new one, I promise."

"It's okay. You don't need to buy anything. Please, though, just be careful."

Raven walked out and Lolo cocked her head to the side. "Bitch," she whispered.

Needing to get the girls away from the house ASAP, I forced them to trim down their shower times, which meant thirty minutes each instead of forty-five. After like a million years (and no more hot water) they were ready for lunch, so I took them to Momma Molson's, because the only thing that could save me was a reliable Fire-Roasted Veggie Salad add chicken hold the cheese.

"Oooh, so sorry," our waiter said, "but we're out of the roasted veggies today."

I reluctantly ordered the Asian salad, dressing on the side. Stacia nodded smugly. "You know what, Jenny? If we had just gone for sushi like Lolo and I planned, we wouldn't have this dilemma. Right, Lolo?"

Lolo buried her face in her oversize Lactaid white chocolate mocha and wouldn't answer. Apparently they'd made plans.

I moaned, "Girls, come on, I was planning for us to have sushi on your last day! I promise!"

Stacia finally ordered. "Okay, okay, I'll have what Jenny's having. No crispy wontons or rice noodles. And dressing on the side." The waiter nodded, holding his tongue.

Lolo eased her face out of the gigantic mug and decided to speak. "Oh my God, it's like so cold here. I can't believe all the snow. It's even worse than Long Island. How do you deal, Jenny?"

"It actually just started getting this way."

"So," Julie said, "how do you like it here?"

"I really like it. I mean—"

But before I could answer, Stacia started sputtering like a windup doll on crystal meth. "Jesus, Jenny, you have to come back home to visit! You won't believe what happened last week at the barbecue and blah blah blah blah blah blah blah blah blah blah blah blah blah blah blah blah blah!"

"I—"

"Blah blah blah blah blah blah blah blah blah blah blah blah blah blah blah blah blah blah blah blah blah blah blah blah blah blah blah blah blah blah blah blah blah blah blah blah blah blah blah blah blah blah blah blah blah blah blah blah but whatev. I'm so good to him. So good to him. It's like if he keeps complaining I'll move on and he can totally miss out for being such an asshole. And we're not like, you know, boyfriend and girlfriend."

"I hate the way he talks to you," Julie said.

"I know, right? Whatever. If he keeps it up then it'll end before it even began. Holla."

I wanted to kill them all.

Then Julie blurted it out: "Josh Beck."

"What?" I said. Of course they'd mention him. He was from our town.

Julie's eyes were wide. "We totally forgot about Josh Beck. Can you believe it? I can't believe what he did. It's so heinous."

"I know," Stacia agreed. "He was so hot, too. It's tragic. I cried when I heard. But Jenny doesn't like to talk about it, Julie."

Julie leaned in. "Did you know him, Jenny? You know, when he died?"

Luckily, I didn't have to answer that because Lolo switched the topic to more important things. "Oh, I almost forgot. Jenny, you have cable, right?"

"Yeah, why?"

"*The Hills* is on tonight."

"That show sucks, Lolo."

"Whatever. I don't care if it's BS."

"Yeah . . . ," Veronica muttered. She wasn't speaking much, and she looked kind of pale the whole time. She just moved her chopped salad around the plate, and I noticed her bites were scarce.

What was keeping you so thin, Veronica?

The next day was the big Juicy Couture warehouse sale. At the break of dawn we piled into Julie's Range Rover and plowed through the snowy roads to Dollard, Quebec. Thank God Chloe passed because I really didn't want her to see the annual "Running of the JAPs."

There seemed to be two types of girls in line: JAPs and skanks. By skanks I mean girls with glitter lipstick, sun-in hair, and like fake boobs. They always had part of their butt crack showing in Miss Sixtys that were a size too small, and they talked as if they probably started kindergarten at age nine. They used real sugar and half and half in their coffee. They were generally nice, though, and were much less aggressive than JAPs when it came to shopping.

"Dammit!" hollered Stacia. "I knew we should've camped out!"

Lolo assured her, "Don't worry, babe. There will be plenty to go around."

And there was. Too much to go around, in fact. The doors opened and the first fifty girls rushed in like some shopping militia mounting an attack. Except the militia had no organization and everyone turned on one another.

There was grabbing for clothes, even a little fighting. I'll admit it, I too couldn't control myself. Everything I saw that looked pretty I grabbed. It was dirt cheap. So what if I ended up spending more money than I would on a normal shopping day? That was the point.

Besides, compared to my friends I was playing it minimalist. I mean, to give you an idea of how they were doing, the girls each pushed a full shopping cart and had camisoles and bathing suits slung through their arms and over their shoulders.

Lolo stormed the aisles, clothes in one hand, cell phone in the other. "I don't see it, Mom, I don't see it!"

I came upon Julie and Stacia on the verge of a spat.

Julie: "You're not gonna get that shirt, are you?"
Stacia: "Uh, yeah, that's why it's in my cart."
Julie: "That's cool. I mean, it's a cool shirt. But I totally picked out the same one and . . . you know . . . I picked it first."

Stacia: "I've had this since like the first ten minutes, Julie. I definitely had it first."

Julie: "Well, I don't wanna get mine if you're getting the same one."

Stacia: "Then don't."

Julie: "But I really like this shirt."

Stacia: "Then buy it!"

Julie: "Okay."

Stacia: "You're really gonna buy it?"

Julie: "Yeah, why?"

Stacia: "I don't know. I just don't think it would look good on you."

Julie: "You're just saying that because you don't want me to buy it!"

Stacia: "No, I'm not. If you like it, go ahead. I'm just saying, it makes you look kinda fat."

Julie: "Thanks! I wish I could be skinny like Veronica, but I actually eat salad!"

Stacia: "Julie, I'm not saying you're fat, just that the shirt makes you look, you know, bigger than you are."

Julie: "I can't believe you just said that. Watch my cart."

She should've known better than to run off like that, leaving Stacia with her stuff.

As Julie went somewhere to cry, Stacia casually swiped the shirt in question and stuffed it under a pile of hooded sweatshirts.

She picked through the rest of the cart while Julie was still gone. "Holla," she muttered.

They were such bitches! I couldn't wait to leave. Oh, there was that Juicy sweater I always wanted!

That night at Hippie Hall the clash of cultures resumed. After every one of my former friends took her second thirty-minute shower of the day, there was no hot water left. None. Anywhere in Montreal. This really bothered the hippies, who often enjoyed nothing more than a warm bath in the dirty tub at the end of their day.

Eventually, Forest (a weirdo with a hippie's name) and Raven dragged me into the basement for a little meeting.

"Jenny, we love you, but I don't know if we can handle your friends," Forest said gently.

"They're driving me fucking crazy!" Raven said less gently.

"You guys, I am so sorry about them. They aren't really my friends—"

"Then what the fuck are they doing here?!" barked Raven.

"Their parents are friends with mine. It's all Long Island stuff. I want them to leave as bad as you do."

"Forest and I—all the girls here—are near boiling point, Jenny. As housemother, you have my permission to go out for as long as you want. And if you *don't* leave, and they keep up this attitude and reckless behavior in *our* home, then I'll use their fancy clothes to wipe my fancy ass."

Raven's tone, paired with the coldness of the basement, made me feel totally isolated. The hippies didn't like me. The weirdos didn't like me. The JAPs didn't understand me. It felt like even Chloe was slipping away, because I hadn't seen her since the invasion.

I considered moving. Freshman dorms weren't *that* bad. Meanwhile, upstairs I could hear Lolo's distinct whine. "Oh my God, this is like the grossest dog I've ever seen!"

Raven turned an angry shade at the mention of Orion. I swore to her and Forest that I'd amend the situation. The question was how.

When I reached my bedroom, Stacia gave me the answer. "So, Jenny, are we gonna like party or what?"

"Yes. We are definitely going out tonight."

Chapter NINETEEN

DON'T DRINK AND KILL

While I expected nothing but complaints when the girls arrived at Ditch Molson, their reaction was totally the opposite. "This is so cool," Lolo declared. "Montreal, here we come." Still, I was prepared for them to flip out about ruining their designer miniskirts, so I brought along a garbage bag with the legs and arms punched out.

"Holla!" chanted Stacia as she climbed into the suit. If she said that one more time I was going to strangle her with the drawstrings. Instead I merely sighed. For a ruthless killer, I was still so powerless around my old friends.

One by one each girl crawled her way through the ditch, took off the giant black garbage bag, and passed it on. It was like watching them transform from California Raisins into *Rich Girls*.

Then it was Edgar's turn. Yes, I'd decided to take Edgar along to both fulfill my promise and provide myself with someone I could stand. Plus, maybe if the girls saw me hanging with a nerd they'd never want to visit me again. Unfortunately, that too didn't work out in my favor. They *loved* Edgar.

"Edgar, you're so cute!" Stacia said as he scooted under the wall. He did look especially cute in a garbage bag for some reason. "I wanna like take you home!"

"That can be arranged," he replied. The girls were cracking up. Why were they only cool when no hippies were around?

PS, Edgar was my second choice. Before leaving, I'd pleaded with Chloe to come with, but she said she was hanging out with Stefan that night. They'd grown totally close and were definitely gonna have sex any minute now, I swear. Still, I had the feeling that Chloe's plans might have been made up to avoid my ex-friends.

We started the night on St. Laurent, but all the lame bouncers were checking IDs. Edgar was the only one who had a fake. Talk about irony—he never even went out.

So for a while we just hung out on the streets, where it was pretty crowded, but as the night wore on we grew more and more impatient. The repeated denials were making the girls whine and my stomach sink. I hated to admit it, but I could've totally used a Perkathingy.

Instead, I ran into Tim Horton's for a frozen cappuccino with skim milk. When I returned, Veronica popped up with some guy on her arm. He was dark and okay-looking and obviously Jewish. She shouted, "This is Richard! He's a sophomore at the . . . uni?"

"McGill!" McGill was this huge university in Montreal.

"He says there's a house party over on Saint . . . Dennis?"

"*St. Denis* and Mont-Royal. You girls wanna come?"

Why not? Whatever dragged the night on and kept these girls away from Hippie Hall.

The house might as well have been a fraternity. Every crevice reeked of beer, and there must've been like a million cans scattered among three floors. It was one of those totally clustered parties where you as a guest had absolutely no idea whose place it was.

As luck would have it, there were like tons of hot Jewish guys there. Stacia and the girls were liquored up by this point and bringing out their "A" game. They had these dweebs refilling their cups, walking them to the bathroom, just fawning all over them. If I was lucky they'd all find someone to go home with.

Edgar was having the time of his life. When my former friends weren't Jew hunting, they flirted with him, danced with him, even covered his face with lip-glossed kisses! It kind of reminded me of the better times I'd had in Long Island, when these girls weren't sounding like outtakes from *My Super Sweet 16*.

Well, whatever. I'd more than fulfilled my bargain—Eddie was in heaven. And he couldn't yell at me for not holding his hand all night the way he'd wanted, because the girls were doing it for me.

As for me, I played the corner and kept out of everyone's way. Sipping on a Molson Export, I kept my mouth shut while this totally sour feeling wouldn't leave. It was like sometimes I could crush the entire house with my fist, other times I was the weakest person there. I was polarized and confused.

It was only after I saw my beer was empty that I realized I'd been drinking way too much. I was pretty drunk, but it might have been a good thing. I finally started to loosen up, and conveniently, a guy approached me.

"Hi there," he said, and extended his hand. "Name's Buddy."

He was pretty hot. Handsome and dark. Probably Jewish. Not too tall. Just old enough. "I've been watching you," he said. "You haven't been talking to anyone, eh?"

"I'm here keeping an eye on my drunk friends."

"Which ones are those?"

"Two of them are over there."

"Oh, Lolo and Julie?"

"Right . . ."

"Cool girls. So you're Jewish, eh?"

"Yep."

"C'est cool. I couldn't tell. With them I could."

"What gave it away? The matching Tiffany's bracelets?"

"I think it was the way their eyes lit up when I said I was
 e-med."

"I'm surprised one of them didn't try to marry you. I'm
   ."

      nny, it's a pleasure. I was just telling your friends how much
         ese parties."

           ere you are."

"Well, how else do I meet a girl like you? You're all students at the uni, right?"

I nodded, milking a lie the girls must've started. And I don't know why, but he made me smile. I could totally see myself making out with him for fun, or lack of anything else to do.

He grabbed my hand. "Come with me, I want to show you something."

He brought me to the top floor, to this room where a bunch of guys were hanging out. The room was like an island getaway compared to the ruckus downstairs. The music was softer. There was a spacious couch and lounge lighting. Last, but certainly not least, was the killer bar with bottles of Grey Goose and Patrón. Nice touch.

Buddy introduced me to his buddies (Ha! . . . sorry), and they all seemed pretty cool. They made me a Grey Goose vanilla soda and it was like total VIP. I think I found my favorite drink of all time that night. Relishing that sweet vanilla taste, I sank into the couch, with Buddy taking the armrest next to me.

We talked more and laughed. Somehow I'd entered this totally giddy mode where it was okay to relax. The girls couldn't touch me here. The murders were far away.

"Close your eyes," Buddy said. I did. He took my hand and began crawling his fingers along my upturned arm. "Tell me when I reach your elbow." It was an old trick, but I liked the way it felt.

"Okay . . . now!" I said. I wasn't even close. Then somehow

Buddy was giving me this pretty good massage. Pretty good because when Svetlana at this place Tonic was your standard, anything less was totally subpar. But I let it take me away. Away from the girls, away from life . . .

"Hey, it's my friend Jenny!" No. No no no! I knew that voice.

"Oh . . . *hey*, Veronica."

It was her alone. Her presence infuriated me. I wanted to tell her that if she left now, she would never suffer the wrath. She'd never have to pay for what she did to me. Mark Leibowitz was gonna ask me to prom and she stole him. Now she was stealing away my little paradise. I was willing to forgive if she just left this very minute.

Obviously that wasn't her intention, though. She plopped down on a chair next to us, and it suddenly seemed really overcrowded. She was drunk too, and within the next few minutes she made up for all the reservations she'd shown up to that point. "Hey, Jenny, did you know I got my belly button pierced?"

Before I could speak like three guys jumped on it. "Let's see it, baby!"

So Veronica slid up her cute little shirt to show all the guys her cutesy-wutesy little belly. I'd like to take this moment to explain something. I was never *that* skinny. I mean, I was never fat or big-boned or anything, but let's just say I was a little self-conscious about my body. I always had been. Great, now you'll think I'm fat. No, I've always been thin with love handles, and a lot of guys actually seem to like it.

But when some ultraskinny head case starts showing off her flat tan gut in front of me in a room full of guys, it doesn't do anything for my self-esteem. It was literally her one edge on me. I should've lifted my shirt and flashed them. That would've gotten their attention. Her kiwis had nothin' on my cantaloupes. Instead I merely sat back and watched the Veronica show.

"You guys are hot!" she hollered—or excuse me, "holla"ed.

She really worked the room. After guzzling back two shots, she practically turned into a stripper, toying with any guy who gave her the time. As she did this, I sank deeper and deeper back into my previous state of mind.

Well at least I still had Buddy, right? Wrong. With my attention diverted, he'd moved into the chair, and Veronica's tiny ass was now firmly planted in his lap. I'm not even exaggerating. They were whispering and giggling with each other.

It was like last year of high school all over again. Every emotion, every bit of anger from prom weekend had been carefully preserved and was now resurfacing.

Except I wasn't pushover Jenny Green anymore. I was fierce, murdering Jenny Green now. Now I was Supergirl. And that stupid hoochie mama was crossing me again!

Ugh, it infuriated me! I know what you're thinking, you despise her as much as I do. Seriously, though, I couldn't kill Veronica.

Buddy patted her thigh. "Hey, let me grab you a drink."

Some guys wandered over to me, but too disgusted to respond, I pointed them in Veronica's direction. "She's promising a free blow job to the guy with the funniest joke," I told them. That sent them running.

It wasn't just Veronica who got under my skin. Buddy, too. I mean, there he was making me feel special, and the second some sluttier girl comes along I'm garbage. I hated that. I hated him!

But I couldn't stop watching him. While part of me despised his being, the other part wanted him back. I wanted him to will himself back to the arm of the couch, where there was a substantial person sitting and not a go-bot with a belly ring.

So I watched him. I watched him go over to the bar and pour Veronica her drink. Then I watched his hand slyly reach into his pocket and pull something out. His movements reminded me of someone. He was sneaky, shady. I could tell he was concealing something in his hand. I thought of Dizzy D.

Then, elusive to everyone but me, Buddy slipped a tiny white pill into Veronica's drink. I saw it. And subtly I watched as he mixed the drink and let the pill dissolve. I couldn't believe my eyes. He was totally trying to date-rape her!

In my head alarms rang, but my body remained motionless. Instead of leaping to Veronica's rescue, I remained seated, trying to calm my outrage.

I couldn't believe this stupid crazy world with these completely amoral people in it! In my head they multiplied. Billions of them scoured the globe, scurrying like rats, decapitating innocent people in some public square, dropping bombs, slipping pills into drinks.

It was unforgivable, and in a matter of seconds I made my

resolve: I'd let Veronica swallow the pill, and by doing so the slate between us was wiped clean. Buddy, however, was an evil bastard. I was sure he'd given her a roofie or whatever that drug was they told us about in health class. This I would not tolerate.

In retrospect, it was the alcohol. The right thing to do was point fingers and call the police. But Supergirl was back as if she'd never left. Supergirl knew the righteous thing was to rid the earth of this human trash.

I waited. The alienation, the discomfort, it was long gone. I observed Buddy keeping tabs on Veronica, waiting for his moment.

He stood. "I gotta take a piss. Veronica, wanna come?"

"I'll wait here, baby." She wasn't under yet. How long did those pills take?

Buddy left the room, and I grabbed my coat. In the pockets were gloves and a hat. They weren't my cheapest, but sometimes a sacrifice must be made. No one noticed as I made my exit—they were too busy paying attention to you know who. I owed her one for that.

I trailed Buddy down two flights of stairs. The line for the bathroom was way too long, so he wandered outdoors. Instantly a plan entered my mind. It was so good I could hardly contain myself.

With Buddy outside, I rushed up the three flights of stairs— and I mean rushed. But I didn't stop at the top floor, where in the nearby room you could hear Veronica's Long Island accent rattling all the windows. Instead I found a doorway leading to the roof and took the short stairway up.

The roof was spacious and filled with random stuff like lawn chairs and hockey equipment. The guys in the apartment probably hung out here a lot in the summer. It worked out for me, because the space granted tons of mobility.

Everything was covered with a blanket of snow and ice. It was windy, too, meaning the footprints would be gone in hours. Normally I would've been freezing cold, but not right now. Right now there was so much energy keeping me warm I could've been wearing my Polo bikini and it wouldn't have mattered.

I acted quickly, leaning over the edge to find Buddy. Peering into the backyard, I saw only a group of smokers. One of them actually looked up. Oh no! I was spotted.

He didn't seem to think much of it, though. Instead of pointing and telling his friends, he merely waved. Stuck, I waved back. I didn't let it deter me. I should have, but I didn't. Too many Grey Goose vanilla sodas in paradise lost.

I ran over to another ledge and looked over. There he was, next to the house, peeing through the frozen chain-link fence. Buddy. There was no one around him. Just someone above him. Supergirl. She thought of Dizzy wandering beneath the apple tree. It made her tingly all over.

The plan was to drop something on Buddy and flatten him into the snow. Looking around, Supergirl saw little that would do the job, and she was losing time. But it took only seconds for everything to click. Hanging off the roof were the biggest icicles in the world. Something out of a Tim Burton movie. Montreal did icicles like nothing you've ever seen, and they were placed perfectly above Buddy's little head.

The only question was how to knock them down. The hockey sticks. She grabbed one among the batch on the roof. It was just right. Light to hold, but strong enough to score a goal in hockey or, say, knock a row of icicles onto Buddy's skull. Down below he was zipping up.

Supergirl crashed the hockey stick against the icicle like she was Wayne Gretsky. It worked like a charm. After three blows the icicle plummeted toward the earth. In her imagination it made a whistling sound, like a bomb dropping.

She moved on to the next icicle. One crack with the hockey stick and down it went. Then the next one. She cleared an entire row of them. Heads up, Buddy!

He looked up just in time to see a gigantic dagger of ice come down on his ugly face. *THUMP!* He crumpled into the snow like an empty can of Molson Import. No sound issued from his distant pale lips. Well, probably no sound. He was kind of far away. She laid the stick back in the pile.

I marveled at her work. I mean, she was really good at what she did. Supergirl, not me. Someone else inside me was doing all this, and she was fantastic at it. Buddy was one less creep in the world. One less adulterer. One less guy who'd be slipping pills into your drink at a party. Next time, Buddy, next time beware the eyes watching you across the room. Beware the woman scorned.

I let the moment swallow me whole. When it passed, I rushed to the door. It was time to get outta there. Twisting the knob, I pulled, but the door didn't move.

Oh, no way. Please don't tell me it was locked!

Stupid! Stupid! Stupid Supergirl! The door was locked! God, I had so little time it was disastrous. I had to get off that roof ASAP. In a frantic daze I sprinted to each ledge and peered over, looking for anything to help. Nothing! Nothing! Nothing! No, it couldn't end like this! My number wasn't up yet!

I ran to the last ledge, the same one I'd just killed Buddy from, hoping there was a detail I'd missed. There was, but my salvation was a good twenty feet away: a second-floor balcony. Ohmigod, it was my only choice. I mean, it was really far, but there was a lot of snow. I couldn't believe I was doing this.

After a brief prayer I climbed onto the ledge. Taking one last breath, I forced myself over and was soon hanging on for dear life. It was slippery, too, like I could go at any moment. Why was I always getting into these stupid situations?

I let go. Down I fell for what seemed like an eternity. Down. Down. Down. I felt my heart roll into my throat. Did I miss the balcony? I didn't! I landed right in a pile of snow! The sweet, cold powder poofed around me in a cloudburst.

Ohmigod, I'd made it. I'd totally made it!

Only after landing did I notice the little glass table I'd

narrowly missed. Phew! I used it for support as I pulled myself to my feet.

Inside the room, the lights were on, but it was empty. If the balcony door wasn't open, I was gonna kick in the glass and hope for the best, but thank God it slid aside with ease. I stepped in and closed the door behind me, then just stood there in the eerie silence.

I took off my gloves and hat and stuffed them into my coat, pulled out my compact and wiped the makeup pad across my T-zone, reapplied my lip gloss, slipped out of my coat and wiped off the leftover snow, then made for the door.

I realized I was limping. My ankle was totally sprained! Well, I'd just have to fight through it for now, and with my teeth clenched I emerged in the hall, walking as normally as I could.

After a few minutes I was spotted by Stacia. "Ohmigawd, Jenny, we've got a major problem. Veronica is so, so wasted. She's upstairs like stripping for the guys. We have to get her out of here."

"But I was having fun."

"Jenny, it's awful. The guys are like taking down their pants. She's gonna start having sex with them soon."

I sighed with delight. "All right. Let's get her home."

On the way home Veronica insisted we eat, so we stopped at a pizza place, where she wolfed down like three slices. As she gorged herself, I knew at some point in the night it'd be coming back up.

Lolo snickered. "You won't believe who Julie made out with tonight."

"Shut up, Lolo. We just kissed!"

"Who?" I asked.

"Edgar!"

I was flabbergasted. "No F-ing way!" Then I was more flabbergasted. "Oh shit! We left Edgar behind!"

How could I have been so stupid! God, it was like my memory was getting worse every day. I guess one could argue that I had other things on my mind. Suddenly I felt really sick. I called Edgar, but he didn't answer, so I texted him saying we needed to leave because of Veronica.

There was no way I was going back to retrieve him. I just hoped he made it out of there before the cops arrived. He called back five minutes later but I didn't answer.

We got back to campus, I took my sweet time rolling Veronica through Ditch Molson, and we finally entered Hippie Hall around four in the morning.

"Ouch!" cried Julie.

"Shhh . . . ," I said.

"I totally bumped my knee. It hurts!"

Big whoop, I thought, *I just broke my ankle.*

The alcohol was wearing off, and late-night wooziness was ∗ping into my soul. I'd done something terrible that night. I 'dn't have killed Buddy. The fear was incalculable. Unfortu-
it was just one of my many problems.

"Julie hurt herself, Jenny," Veronica slurred. "Don't be a bitch!"

"Veronica, please be quiet," Stacia said, taking my back.

But Veronica wouldn't shut up. "Jenny, why are you such a bitch?"

"Jenny, why are you limping?" asked Stacia.

I didn't respond. I had bigger things to deal with, like how would I function tomorrow with all this blood on my hands? Sloppy blood. Blood that could be traced back to me. There was that guy who'd seen me on the roof. Should I find him and kill him, too? No, that was the alcohol talking.

A light turned on. One of the hippies appeared in the hallway. Her name was Cara, and we didn't really know each other. But now she was up. Very politely she asked, "Hey, do you think you girls can keep it down?"

"No!" Veronica replied.

I quickly interfered. "Cara, I'm so sorry. We're going to my room. I promise we won't be loud."

But Veronica persisted. "Oh, we'll be loud! We'll be loud as we wanna be, you Birkenstock-wearing hippie bitch!"

"Veronica, shut the fuck up, I'm trying to call someone."

"Fuck you, Lolo!"

"This way, girls. Come on." Apologizing again to Cara, I led the JAPs upstairs, where doors were opening. Edgar called again, but I couldn't bring myself to talk to him.

Then he texted: THE COPS R HERE!

My teeth were grinding into my fingernails. It was too much!

There were like three hippies up now, Raven being one of them. "Oh, look who's back, the hair-drying queens! Did you come back to shower again? Or maybe I need to write you up for sneaking off campus, Jenny."

That bitch! She gave me permission to leave. But all I said was, "Raven, we're going to bed."

It could've been a civil war if the hippies weren't peace lovers. There was no way I could regain the house's respect after this whole ordeal. Damn, and I thought letting Veronica take roofies was totally sweet. In the end it only bit me in the ass.

Somehow I pacified the pacifists and convinced them we were going to bed. I shuffled the girls into my room. Jacinda wasn't there as always, and I could've made out with her hairy boyfriend for keeping her away.

My ankle was seriously hurting now, but I tried my best to conceal it. I closed the door behind me. "Okay, girls, it's bedtime."

"Fuck you," Veronica gurgled. With half-closed eyelids, she floated in every direction like a buoy on the water.

Stacia was baffled. "Veronica, what is your problem? Jenny didn't do anything to you."

"She took Buddy away."

Oh shit. Veronica had noticed me leaving after Buddy. Had else? This was not good news. Not good news at all. We ess. A biatch, hoochie, pain-in-the-A witness who obvi- like me. "Who's Buddy?" I asked.

lly, Veronica didn't answer. She was too close to

nodding off. Then she remembered something. "Ohmigawd, I ate pizza. I ate like five slices of pizza! I'm totally gonna throw up."

Here it came. I figured she was gonna sprint to the bathroom and make herself throw up, but when her face lurched and her cheeks puffed up, it was clear she intended to vomit right there in the bedroom.

I became a real taskmaster then and pushed her onto Jacinda's futon. It was timed perfectly, and she threw up all over the pretty colors. Now I had an excuse to replace the futon and a reason to yell at Veronica the next day. Oh well, at least some things worked out. It was a lot of throw-up too. Corn, when did she eat corn? Peppers, onions, black olives. Gross.

Veronica passed out in her own vomit. It seemed just. I hoped for zits by morning.

"Ohmigaaawd! Where am I gonna sleep now?!" Julie fretted. She was crying. In fact, everyone was.

Everyone but me . . . and Lolo (who was texting someone). I was too shocked to cry, completely on the fritz. I kept thinking about Buddy's corpse and what clues I'd left behind. There was no way I was getting out of this one—I mean, if drugged, dumb, and drunk Veronica was a witness, who knows how many sober witnesses there were?

It wasn't fair! I was still essentially a virgin and I was totally going to jail! It was so stupid what I did. Careless and stupid. Let this be a lesson to you all: Don't drink and kill.

Chapter TWENTY

THE DAY AFTER

Maybe it was the JAPs who started it. Maybe it was Josh Beck, or the crazy school shooter kid, or maybe it was just this messed-up world in general. It was hard to pinpoint exactly, but it seemed life was moving in fast-forward and the pause button wasn't working.

The morning after Buddy's murder, I awoke with dried tears on my cheeks. When I stepped out of bed I landed right on my bad ankle and dropped to the floor. Ouch! I'd totally forgotten about that.

Veronica was sick all day. I'll admit I felt pretty bad, but it didn't stop me from taking her hundred-dollar check for Jacinda's futon.

As for Buddy, he was a first. I was totally undecided as to whether his death was necessary, so for the first time I experienced what's best described as bona fide guilt. Yes, he did something utterly despicable by drugging Veronica, but was it deserving of the ultimate punishment? If it was innocent Chloe he'd drugged, then the answer would be yes, of course. I'd kill for Chloe.

But then again, say Dizzy had only drugged me and nothing else? Would I have murdered him? Hell no. Still, though, roofies and perk-whatevers were totally different. No, Jenny, don't think about it. But I killed him without mercy! I killed him. No, Supergirl did.

But there was no Supergirl, only me. It was me who'd done those things! But I saved Veronica and many girls in the future from being drugged and raped. Could I simultaneously be a murderer and a hero? I needed some Prof Stone time. Or maybe a shrink.

Anyway, I had two goals that day: convince the girls to help me buy Jacinda a new futon and ensure they didn't catch wind of Buddy's death. Neither would be too difficult, but somewhere in the midst of this we had to shop more, get a massage at Tonic, eat sushi at the Old Port, and help Veronica get well enough to drive home that night. Most importantly, we had to keep every JAP out of every hippie's way.

Things went smoothly for the most part. First was the futon. After cleaning off the vomit, I braced myself, then gave a nod . . . the girls and I flipped it over. "Ohmigawd! There's more. The puke like went through the futon!"

No, Julie, that's actually the over-a-month-old blood from when I stabbed Josh Beck with a bong. I was amazed more didn't stick to the floor, just some flakes that were crusted into the wood, nothing a tough scrub job wouldn't fix. That or a new futon to cover it up.

As moronic as Julie's theory on the futon-penetrating puke was, the girls all seemed to buy it. None of these girls would be getting into NYU, if you catch my drift.

We hauled the blood-and-puke-encrusted mattress down the stairs, passing some hippies who were too angry with us to even look our way. Jeez, they sure knew how to make a girl *with a broken ankle* feel good.

"This futon smells like sewage," noted Lolo. She wasn't really helping much. She just kind of kept her distance, and a look of disgust never left her face. She confided, "My mom would flip if she knew I was in the same room with this lump of garbage." Then it was back to texting on her trusty Sidekick.

Anyway, it took like a million years, but we finally strapped the futon onto the snow-covered SUV. Upon my insistence we drove it all the way to the Montreal dump, and let me tell you, it felt really awesome to finally rid myself of that thing. *Jacinda should be happy,* I thought. Not that I was looking for a thank you, but it would've been nice. PS, we had the girls' parents call the school, and it granted us special off-campus permission for the day. No digging ditches for us!

At the dump they stopped us at the gate and made us throw it in this enormous Dumpster, but I wanted to go inside, just to see where they'd found Josh's body. Sick, right?

Okay, so I know Veronica was like dying, but I convinced the girls that she could wait a little. We stopped at a mattress store, and I picked out this really cool futon that had lots of different colors, which I knew Jacinda would like probably love.

It was almost three by the time we plopped the new futon down. Edgar called again, but I wasn't ready to talk yet.

Veronica was still really sick. "Maybe we should take her to the hospital," Julie suggested.

"No . . . ," Veronica muttered. "I'll be fine."

The girls and I shrugged, then it was off to Tonic!

Somewhere in the middle of my massage, I remembered a nightmare from the night before. I was in a mall, but I wasn't shopping. There was a mirror—in it my face was twisted and my hair a hundred different colors. Then I did laundry, the old-fashioned way, you know, like dipping clothes in this big bucket of water. But instead of those provincial, small-town clothes, it was designer jeans and sweaters. Instead of water, it was blood. It dripped from the clothes hanging on the line. It ran through the cracks in the floor. It covered my hands and arms. I hated blood and it was everywhere.

Anyway, it totally bugged me out and yes, I'll admit Svetlana's hands were still heavenly, but by the time I left Tonic I was stuck in a dark place that was growing only more familiar.

By that evening, Veronica was learning to walk again and

able to hold down fluids. She'd be okay, I thought. Eventually the pale hue of sickness would leave her cheeks and the faithful bronze of her spray-on tan would return.

As the car drove away I was left alone on the curbside. But who was I kidding? I'd been alone their entire visit.

Chapter TWENTY-ONE

THE NIGHT AFTER

I called Edgar an hour after the JAPs departed.

"You abandoned me!"

"Edgar, I'm sorry. I'm so sorry." I just kept saying it. Genuine tears rolled down my cheeks. I was so F-ing sad and I wasn't sure why. "Are you in trouble?"

"The cops weren't busting up the party. Someone died. A McGill student. An icicle landed right on his head! Unreal, eh?"

"Oh my God . . ."

"Listen, I'm on my way to a Science Club meeting. There's just something you need to know. The cops were there, and I was talking freely to a guest. I mentioned your name and two of the cops were suddenly all up in my face. I . . . I told them you'd been at the party."

"You did what?"

"I didn't see the harm! They like knew you or something. It was a stocky, kind of fat cop with a mustache and then a younger, taller one. They were cool, Jenny. They even drove me to Ditch Molson and let me sneak back in. And why are you crying? I had a great time last night. I owe you one, Greenie!"

I shut my phone meditatively. Jacinda walked in then.

"Ummm . . . Jacinda?"

"What's this? Where's my futon?" This wasn't gonna be as easy as the bong.

"About that. I had some girls over these past few days. They left like an hour ago."

"Jenny, what happened? That was like my parents' futon from the sixties. It's been in my family for decades."

"My friend Veronica threw up all over it. So we tossed it and got you a new one!"

"What? Because there was puke on it? So what, Jenny? I've thrown up on that thing a bunch of times. It's got like four generations of puke all over it. But you know what? Puke washes out. It washes out, Jenny!"

"Jacinda, I bought you a new one. See all the nice colors! Puke on those!"

"I didn't want a new one!"

"Well, I'm sorry! There was throw-up on your futon and it was my friend's fault, so I wanted to be nice and buy you a new one."

"Buy me a new one. That's always your solution. I thought you were making progress. I thought maybe you'd become less materialistic. You can't just *buy* forgiveness. I loved that futon."

And here we went again: "Puke or not it can be covered in

snot, but that don't mean it can't rot with me when I'm free to be pissed you materialist!"

"Isn't the futon a material thing, though?"

"It's a place to sleep! It's not a pair of thousand-dollar jeans! It's not a horsepowered hair dryer! It was part of my life, and you just tossed it away!"

Usually I'd cry, but I'd used up my tears on Edgar. Now I almost wanted to laugh. I wasn't normal anymore, and Jacinda was making me nauseous. The sad thing was, we *had* been making progress in our own way.

I just exploded. "I said I'm sorry! What the F! I mean, I thought I was doing the right thing! Fine, Jacinda, I'm a terrible roommate, but you won't have to deal with me anymore! I'm leaving this Hippie Hell that smells like your old, crusty, hairy armpit! So now you're rid of me for life, and all it cost you was your precious futon! God!"

One hour later . . .

"Ummm . . . Daddy?"

"Jenny, it's so good to hear your voice. How was it having your friends in town? How are they?"

"They're okay. Actually, they were all kinda bratty."

"Don't say that about your friends, Jenny."

"It's true, but listen. That's not why I called. Ummm . . . Daddy, can I move?"

"What?"

"I can't live with the hippies anymore. All they do is smoke drugs and have sex and drink all night. I can't concentrate. I'm gonna fail my classes if I don't get out of here. And you said classes were most important."

"But Jenny, the freshman dorms are probably the only thing available."

Whatever. Compared to hippies and weirdos, living with freshmen was practically a luxury.

"Ummm . . . ummm . . . ummm . . . Chloe?" I was running out of breath. We were on the bikes at the gym. We had to switch from the treadmill because of my ankle. The bikes still made it hurt, but it was tolerable (besides, I liked the burn). This was all the same night, if you can believe it.

"What's up?" she asked.

"I want . . . to move."

"Move? Like from . . . Hippie Hall?"

"Yes."

"Wait . . . stop." So we stopped biking. She took a few breaths. Then, "What do you mean, Jenny? You can't leave! I'll have no one to talk to!"

"No. I want you to come with me."

"Oh . . . but the only thing available is the . . ."

Freshman dorms.

Okay, I know I was only sixteen, but if you'd gone through as much as I had this year, you'd feel a lot older than high school freshmen too. God, they were like toddlers uncaged! They constantly trafficked outside the door like it was Mardi Gras or something. On our first day we were assaulted with Silly String. Come on, really?

The resident adviser's name was Ben, and he was like twenty-six and kind of a pain in the A; a real stickler, you know? Raven was much cooler. But with all the crazy freshmen running around, Ben had his hands full, so sneaking out would be a cinch.

Also on the plus side, Chloe and I somehow got adjoining rooms with a shared bathroom. It was nice to be hippie free, but each bedroom was like a quarter the size of our old ones. I insisted on keeping my bed, and between that and my dresser there was only a little sliver of space to walk around. Our bathroom was quaint, but I was happy to share it with my best friend in the world.

As for the moving itself, well, the movers took care of everything. I used the free time to cut a lot of choppy layers in my hair and lighten it with toffee and caramel highlights. It was so Jennifer Aniston.

I hoped changing locations would change me, but deep down I knew better. I was just killing time before I was caught or before I did something crazy, and it didn't matter where I slept. I was losing control. But did I ever have control? Who was it who slept here? What had she done with the naive jappy girl who first occupied this bed?

The news of Buddy's death took a while to hit the press. Why they kept it a secret for so long was a mystery to me, and the articles didn't alleviate any concerns. Everyone said the death was presumed to be accidental, but an investigation was still launched. I just kept picturing that kid who waved to me from the backyard. He must have said something.

Some cops suspected it was foul play. It was.

In the early morning hours, after sleep was no longer an option, I'd repeat to myself over and over again: "My intentions are good. My intentions are good. My intentions are good. . . ."

Chapter TWENTY-TWO

WERE MY INTENTIONS STILL GOOD
IF I KILLED A POLICE OFFICER?

I entered Prof Stone's office a cold shell of a person. He noticed immediately.

"Jenny, what's wrong?" He walked over to me, hugging me with his thin but sturdy arms. A hug from my prof. It made me warm all over, kind of. "Tell me what's bothering you, princess. I hate when a student's upset, especially a girl like you."

I'd been staring aimlessly. Prof Stone couldn't figure it out. He poked me with his cane to force a smile. My dry lips parted, "I've changed this year. It's like part of me is dying."

"We all shed our youth at some point. But don't think of it as dead. It will always be a part of you."

"Prof Stone, why do we have to invade Iraq? America, I mean. Why do we have to bomb houses?"

"To protect yourselves."

"But some people say it was our presence in the Middle East that caused all this. Before 9/11. That we were setting up military bases on holy grounds. That we've been drilling for oil without regard for the people whose land we're on. Isn't that an invasion of *their* territory? What makes America the supreme judge of things?"

"Right. And what made Rome the supreme judge of things, or Great Britain? Power did. And power can be ugly. It can be blind."

"But who's right, then?"

"Whoever does the most good with the power they obtain, I suppose."

"Everyone makes mistakes, though."

"Everyone's human."

"Then how can one human decide he's more powerful than the next?"

"Jenny . . . it's in their nature. Look at the animals. Alpha wolves, lion kings. They don't question why they are who they are, they just make the most of it. They do what their bodies and minds tell them to do. They do what their genes tell them to do. Yes, in a perfect universe no single human is more powerful than the next. But in our universe, a human *is* more powerful than the next, he's smarter than the next, *she's* smarter than the next, *she's* prettier than the next. It's the way it is. Is it the way it will always be? Who knows?"

"What is it you genuinely believe in, Prof Stone?"

"I believe in love, Jenny. All else is secondary. Love drives the world. Not power."

"That's funny. All the pretty girls love a guy with power and money. That's not true love."

"Even when it's a lie, love is true when you believe it is."

Believing a lie. Or better yet, accepting something that might be completely false. Why did I feel like that was such an important step toward adulthood?

You're not going to believe what happened next.

I was still thinking about lies, intentions, and murder on my way to AP Calc. They occupied my mind so much that I almost smacked right into . . . Officer Perv! He was dressed in uniform.

"Hey there," he said, trying to sound dark.

"Hi Jim. Or is it Tim?" I was already fuming, for some reason.

"Don't know what you're talking about, eh?"

"What do you want?" I snapped.

"Nothing. You should get used to seeing me around campus, though."

"Trying to meet more underclassmen, I guess."

"Nice one. I'm tailing a suspect, actually."

"Huh. I didn't think you had the *balls*," I snickered.

Okay, obviously I should've cowered at his suspect remark, but he just seemed so . . . weak. His lips moved, but no words emerged. His face was beet red. I wanted to knee him in the balls all over again. Instead I headed to class and left him digging for a comeback. Thank God my limp was pretty much gone by now. Would it have been a clue?

When I sat down at my desk, the nerdy teacher gave me a very warm look. I guess he was happy I finally showed up (I'd been flaking on class lately). Whatever, Teach, cherish the moment. I was only here because I'd used up all my absences and then some.

It took a good five minutes after the bell for me to register that class had even begun. For a while I just zoned out, biting every nail until it hurt. Finally I reached into my backpack and pulled out my notebook. Along with it, however, came a note. It dropped onto the floor.

I scooped it up and opened it. Ready for this? Here's what it read: *I know who you are.*

I imagined all the places my backpack had been that day, but Prof Stone's office was all I could think of. Who wrote this? One of the hippies? Officer Perv? No, he was too goofy to pull something like this off.

Edgar. It had to be Edgar. He was sitting right next to me. We both looked up at the same time, and he nerdily winked hello in that too-cute-to-be-cool way. It definitely *wasn't* Edgar.

Then who?

Chapter TWENTY-THREE

FROM BAD TO WORSE

As Chloe helped decorate my room, I saw it next to the door: a small folded piece of paper. Somehow I just knew what it was, and I scurried over before Chloe could see it. I unfolded it: *You're not fooling anyone, Jenny.*

I totally wanted to vomit. Maybe if I'd been sleeping more it wouldn't have made me so crazy, but I lusted for the murder of this secret admirer (or whatever you want to call him).

"What's that?" Chloe spotted me reading the same sentence a hundred times. Was it her writing these?

"Oh this, I don't know. One of the movers must have dropped it."

"Jenny, I know this place sucks, but I'm excited for some reason. We can make this fun!"

"I know, babe. We'll just have to be creative." From the hallway came the distinct blare of an air horn. "Very, very creative."

Chloe laughed, buying my joke. It was easy to sell. I was no longer conflicted in my acting.

By the way, Chloe and Stefan, as I think I mentioned earlier, were getting totally serious. He was super cool, and my only concern was whether he cheated, but Chloe convinced me of his monogamy.

And they were really, really in love with each other. They did those corny things that only people in love could do, like sharing ice cream cones or taking long walks around a pond. And I guess they hadn't done the deed yet, but it was coming any day now. I just prayed it wouldn't be in her dorm room, where I might be able to hear it. The last thing I wanted to hear was Chloe in the throes of passion, fully satisfied, in love.

I read the note again. Now who *wasn't* I fooling? He would be my next victim. And if I didn't find him, I'd find someone else.

My intentions were good. My intentions were good.

It was a week before American Thanksgiving, and I was in Prof Stone's lecture. He assigned us our paper for the midterm. "Okay, class, I have a special opportunity for you all. On your next paper, I want you to be as free as a naked child fresh out of the womb. Your topic: whatever you wish. Your length: whatever you desire. Make it good, though. I want to be educated. Teach me something. I want to read every line with rabid interest." He looked at me and grinned eagerly. The bell rang.

Exiting the building, I threw a quick glance over my shoulder. I saw a car lurking between the trees. An old brown Lincoln. Officer Perv was at the wheel, watching me from behind steel-colored shades.

But if Officer Perv had anything on me, he'd take me in for questioning. You had nothing, Officer Perv. Nothing.

Chapter TWENTY-FOUR

NEO-MORON

I received two more notes that same week, one in my mailbox, the other right in my pocket. This guy was good.

The first one read: *I'm just like you.*

So that's why he wasn't calling the cops. He was a killer too. There were other murderers—it was a city, after all.

The truth was, though, he was nothing like me. There was no one like me. Ninjas, maybe. But not him. If he was a killer, he did it with no code. No honor. He killed because he wanted to watch his victims suffer. It disgusted me, and I hoped to meet him so he could be my next victim. I couldn't think of anything more satisfying than killing a cold-blooded, vicious killer.

My prayers were answered with the note in my pocket: *Meet me at the fountain at two p.m.*

Well, that settled it. I was totally meeting this guy.

So at two in the afternoon on November 15, I waited by this big fountain in the heart of Molson Academy. I was already wearing a cheap hat and gloves and an old coat I never wore. PS, the gloves were kind of a pain because I really wanted to chew my fingernails.

Finally this gangly guy with glasses and dandruff-ridden hair approached me. He was ten minutes late. I hated tardiness.

"Hello, Jenny," he said. From five feet away I could smell his dragon breath. I mean, this guy was really gross. I recognized him too, from one of my classes. I'm pretty sure it was AP Calc. Oh, and he sounded American. "You showed. So we are alike. Come with me."

He led me away from the fountain. I didn't even know his name yet.

I was careful to avoid eye contact with anyone as we strolled away. Apparently this freak didn't want to be seen either, since he walked briskly and kept his eyes to the ground. Nowhere in sight was Officer Perv, but if he was lurking somewhere, then this was my final undoing.

Freakboy led me to a big house that was actually somewhat close to Hippie Hall. I couldn't remember the name, but it wasn't as nice as the others. We snuck in through a back door and up to his room.

The room was messy and bare at the same time. There were newspapers strewn about and a small, old-school television on a chair. The only place to sit was atop these big cement blocks. On the wall was a poster of someone I recognized but whose name escaped me. I want to say Joseph Stalin. It was safe to say there was no roommate.

Anyway, the mysterious boy spread his arms in welcome. "What do you think?"

"What's your name?"

"Thomas. Thomas Baker." Half-baker was more like it.

"Thomas?" I asked. "How do you know about me?"

"I can just tell, Jenny. I can just tell when there's another one of us."

"Us being . . ."

"Don't play games. I've been watching you. I'm so proud of you."

"Proud of me?"

"It's not easy for one to see the shame of her own kind. The empty gossip. The mockery. The vapid, shallow passing of time. You are strong to admit you're weak," he continued.

I didn't show my hand. "How could you tell, though? That I was different."

"When I see you, your eyes are always distant. They're cold, too. You're filled with conflict and hate. You have a killer inside you, correct?"

"Maybe."

"You do. And I've been sent to draw it out. We'll be famous." He glanced to the window, as if there was an audience out there just waiting for him to do something stupid. He pondered aloud, "To think you were on the list. It would have been a grave mistake. I've compiled a new one."

It all caught up to me then. The school shooter kid. Harrison something. It looked like they hadn't caught everyone involved. Thomas Baker was yet another school shooter.

Now if the old Jenny Green were here, she'd flee for her life. He was totally creeping me out! I mean, I know this all sounds like some weird dream or something, but he was real, and he was a soulless being—a vessel of hate that this overpopulated world didn't need.

He handed over a sheet of paper. It was filled with names.

"I want to show you something important." He reached into his closet and withdrew a shoebox. He pulled out a very old dagger that was in really nice condition. It was sharp and curved. On the handle was a swastika. "It's from the Second World War. I got it on eBay."

"Can I hold it?"

"Be very gentle."

He handed it over just as I saw a name on the list: Edgar Barnes. My Edgar? Was Barnes his last name? Even if it wasn't the same Edgar, I was sent into a rage.

I held the dagger in my hands. The moment was ripe. Thomas Baker was not worthy of reproduction. He was not worthy of life. I raised the dagger. Sunlight bounced off the shiny silver as I advanced.

Thomas was facing the closet, retrieving some other heinous weapon, I bet. When he turned, I brought the dagger down on his small, black heart. I brought it down again and again. His back arched reflexively from the impact. Then he crumbled. He was too weak to fight me.

Okay, you know I hate blood, so I'm gonna skip ahead a little. . . .

Thomas collapsed to the floor. Dead.

Across the room there was a big plastic bag with toiletries in it just sitting on the floor. Don't ask me why, but I emptied the bag and threw in the dagger, then put it in my coat. A souvenir, I guess. A reminder. There was no escaping who I was this time, and I wasn't gonna let myself try.

I left the building as inconspicuously as I'd come.

After wading through like a herd of freshmen to reach my room, I collapsed into bed and took out the dagger, leaving it in the bag. I stroked the blade through the plastic, not looking, though, because of the blood. Totally twisted, I know. Once finished, I shoved the dagger into my own shoe box and set it on the top shelf of my closet.

Slamming the closet door shut somehow opened in me all the emotions I'd been suppressing. I couldn't deal. I raced to the bathroom and found a small bottle of Advil, half-full. I shoveled the pills into my mouth and forced myself to swallow them all.

Half an hour later came intense sickness. Lots of throwing up. I was gonna die and I was glad. Life was hopeless. I'd never make it in this world. I'd never have amazing sex with Prince Charming. I'd never get married or be a famous actress or raise however many kids.

It was time to end all this misery. It was time for Jenny Green to say good-bye to this cruel, chaotic existence.

PART THREE

A Princess Finds Her Prince

Chapter TWENTY-FIVE

A SUPER-WHACKED-OUT
JENNY GREEN THANKSGIVING

I died. Just kidding. Obviously I didn't die.

Seriously, though, it was a miracle I didn't kill myself the day I killed Thomas Baker. In fact, it was pretty miraculous I didn't kill myself in the days following.

Half my waking hours were devoted to the same questions over and over again: How would I do myself in? Where? Razor blades in the bathtub? Too cliché, too bloody. Jump from a moving helicopter? Too expensive, too much of a hassle. Drink all my toenail polish? I didn't even know if that killed you, and I didn't want another night like with the Advil. Yuck.

The media was in a frenzy on campus that week. I mean, *two* potential school shooters in one year, *two* deaths—it was a bit much. Dean Sanders did a lot of apologizing and promised to amp up security in the months to come. He wasn't very convincing, though. Parents withdrew their kids in droves, although school stayed in session. I considered finding out what opened up in terms of housing but didn't have the energy. It was a total disaster.

There was a campuswide search for the missing dagger that had killed Thomas Baker. The police were checking every room and house. In anticipation, I ran to the woods and actually climbed a tree, taping the plastic bag to the top side of a branch.

Later that day, who should show up at my door but Officer Prick and Officer Perv. Bearing suspicious glares, they searched my room up and down, naturally finding not a thing. I retrieved the dagger two days later. I just couldn't part with it.

By then I didn't feel like committing suicide so much anymore. I mean, I hadn't acted in vain; I'd acted with purpose. If I hadn't murdered Thomas Baker, then he would have like gunned down a whole bunch of people who definitely didn't deserve it.

The idea chased away enough demons to keep me alive, but plenty of demons remained. They clawed at me every minute. They glared at me every time I saw Officer Perv's car tailing me to class. I think I just wasn't cut out for the whole killing business.

Through all this, it was Chloe who kept me somewhat sane, as she had all those times before at Hippie Hall. She became my link to the real world. Instead of devoting any more time to murder, I tried to focus on our friendship and on her relationship with Stefan.

So every night when Chloe came back to the dorm, I'd rush into her room with two soy chai lattes and get the 411: Had she and Stefan done it yet? When would it happen?

Her stories reminded me of life's joys and pleasures, despite all the mania. Chloe seemed genuinely in love, and maybe one day I too would have that naive look in my eyes.

Thanksgiving was the big day for her. It wasn't like she and Stefan mapped it out, but she just knew somehow that it was the night. She even got permission from Ben, the RA, to step out. PS, the fact that it was Thanksgiving had nothing to do with it—Stefan could care less about our American holiday. The Canadians had their own version earlier in the fall. Anyway, I wanted to be happy for Chloe, but deep down inside I was pretty depressed about it.

You're probably wondering why I was in Montreal on Thanksgiving and not at home with my loving family. I just didn't have the strength to face them. Like the ice on my windowpane, I was frozen. Plus, I'd seen them last month on Visiting Day. I know, you're wondering why I didn't mention it. But what do you want me to say? They came, they ate, you wouldn't have cared.

My parents were like bugging out about Thomas Baker and just everything, but I assured them I was safe. It took forever, but I assured them. Then I explained how much work I had, and they guaranteed a Thanksgiving feast with all my relatives when I came back. How sweet. I wanted to cry. For now, though, it was just soy chai lattes and good old TCBY. Thank God for that store on campus.

All right, I'll come clean, there were some hobbies during the Jenny Green super-whacked-out depression era that I wasn't gonna mention. The least embarrassing was my new clothing line. Wearing gloves, I used the Thomas Baker dagger to shred my designer clothes. The result: *Dramacide*. Long story short: Dramacide will not be hitting a store near you anytime soon.

The second least embarrassing hobby was cutting. Many times when I thought about suicide, I'd make a pretty deep cut in my forearm. I'd close my eyes so as not to see the blood and let the pain jolt my entire body. I know, it sounds gross and weird, but there was something cathartic about it.

Then there was the mouse. I saw it in the hallway when no one else was around. In a frenzy I chased it down until it was cornered, then squished it with my bare foot. Crunch! Ugh, just mentioning it now brings back a kind of unprecedented guilt; I mean, it was just a poor little mouse. There were other things like that, but I'm getting nauseous, so moving on . . .

On Thanksgiving night I found some red wine. Like a lush, I drank straight from the bottle and got drunk alone. It was a big mistake. About halfway through I held up my compact mirror and reveled in my red lips and tongue. For perhaps the only time in my life, I missed the sight of blood.

The lust was back. The lust to kill. Anyone. One of those annoying freshmen maybe. Or better yet, kill myself . . . again.

Around two in the morning I wasn't drunk anymore, just dazed. I don't think I'd moved the entire night. The idea of ending it all left me paralyzed.

Then I did move. There were knives in the dorm kitchen down the hall. I left my room and proceeded slowly, methodically, unsure whether to use them on myself or someone else. I grabbed the biggest knife I saw.

Keys jingled out in the hallway then, followed by a heavy sigh. I knew that sigh. Chloe. She saved me yet again just by coming home, and for the first time that night I noticed I was breathing. I fixed my hair and wiped my cheeks in case there were tears, dropped the knife, and put on my best-friend face.

I appeared in her doorway, startling her. "Jesus, Jenny! Didn't think you'd be up. Happy Thanksgiving!"

"Thanks, Chlo. Well?"

"Well . . ."

"Well, what happened?"

"Okay, give me a sex. I mean, sec."

"Ooohh! You totally did it!" I knew my Freudian slips.

"Hold on, Jenny!"

I planted myself on her bed as she took off her coat and went to the bathroom. I swear, the longer she took the more genuinely thrilled I was. Well, actually, it's hard to say that thrilled was the only word. There was jealousy, too. Maybe I just wanted her to get the story over with. Deep in my heart, though, I was happy for her. I would've been a little happier if I had a story to match, but whatever.

Anyway, she finally emerged from the bathroom and plopped down next to me. She was totally trying to hide her smile, but I could tell the deed was done.

Here it came: "Jenny, we totally did it."

"Ohmigod!!!" We giggled like kids and hugged. "Tell me everything, but leave out the gross parts."

"It's a fairly long story."

"Wait a second. Why are you here? Why didn't you sleep there, Chlo?"

"I'll get to that."

"Right. First the sex."

"The sex. Right. Well, we both knew it was the night. I Ditched Molson and Stefan took me out to this amazing place for dinner."

"Where?"

"Queue de Cheval."

"C'est cool."

"It was *soooo* delicious. Then it was back to his place. He'd totally cleaned it up. It was immaculate, Jenny. And he'd put scented candles all around the apartment, so there was like this, you know, vanilla smell to the air. And the lights were perfectly dim. Everything was so lucid and open, you know. Then we watched a movie."

"Which one?"

"*Titanic.*"

"Nice and long."

"And a great movie."

"The best."

"I know, Leo's so cute in it. Anyway, right after we see the boat, Stefan gets really close to me. He smells nice too. Oh, by the way, we had oysters for dinner, and they're like an aphrodisiac, so I was totally horny." As Chloe said this she inched closer, as if re-enacting Stefan's motions. "And he looks me in the eye and says for the first time, 'Chloe, I love you.' I melted."

"Wow."

"I know, right? Then we just went at it. And he like swooped me off my feet, literally, and took me into the bedroom. There were more candles. He put on some music. It was like this soft, jazzy music. Totally helped. God, Jenny, I was practically wet already."

"Chloe, holy shit!"

"I know! But listen, so he tells me the first time might hurt because, you know, I'm a virgin, but instead of hesitating I just said, 'Bring it on.'"

"Bring it on?"

"Bring it on. And he did. Jenny, he started slow, he knew everywhere to touch me. He said the most passionate things."

"Did you . . . ?"

"Well, here's why I'm home right now. The answer is . . . no. I felt many great things. Many great things. The whole experience was nothing but wonderful. But I didn't climax. I know I said that thing about being wet, but I didn't climax, even though I should have. And after it was over I realized something. Jenny, you're gonna have to brace yourself for this. Are you braced?"

"Yes!"

"I think I'm a lesbian."

"What?!!!!"

"Or maybe bi. I don't know. I'm serious, Jenny! I mean, you know I used to fool around with girls in Jersey, but what I never told you was how much I enjoyed it. And the whole night was so amazing, but there was something missing. He touched me in all the right places, and I realized it wasn't the location that was wrong, it was the hand. It was the touch. It lacked something. It lacked a woman's grace, a woman's understanding. And I don't know, the other day in class my teacher was reading from this book by Patricia Highsmith about these lesbians—"

"*The Price of Salt*?" I said, naming the book.

"Huh? Jenny, don't ask me about food at a time like this. I don't know, five bucks a kilo?"

"No, Chlo—"

"Just listen. She was reading from that book, and something in me awakened. I mean, those words turned me on. I need some time to be with girls. I mean, *really* be with girls . . ."

Suddenly I noticed that Chloe had inched even closer. I mean, she was practically in my lap. And I'll be honest, if there was a lesbian moment in my life, it was this one here. I wanted to be loved and understood more than ever. God, everything was so twisted, if Chloe had just leaned in and gone for it I probably would've given the okay. Instead, though, she looked into my eyes, as if reading me, and the moment passed.

I went to Chloe's mini-fridge for some water. "But Chloe, I don't get it. You seem all happy right now."

"I am. I've rediscovered myself."

"More like reinvented."

"That too! And it feels great! A whole new world awaits me. A world of women. Hey, grab me a Diet Snapple, will ya?"

"But are you happy?"

"I'm excited. It was taking that first step. That was the hardest part . . . oooh! Diet Peach Tea, thanks!"

I was blown away. For once I was entirely absorbed in every word she said. I mean, she was a lesbian. I didn't know any lesbians, you know, except all the weirdo lesbians at Hippie Hall, but they didn't really count. "Is this gonna change anything between us?"

"Only if we have sex. Kidding! No, why would it? Unless you have a problem with gays."

"Of course not. I'm so proud of you."

"I'm sure I'll be a mess come morning. But tonight was like a dream. I had the best sex I'll ever have with a man, and it's like it prepped me for sex with a woman. That'll be the ultimate level."

She'd inspired me. I mean, come on, if Chloe could reinvent herself, I totally could, too. No more murder. No more starvation and stress. It wasn't the real me. The real me was a young Jewish girl in search of the perfect man.

It was time to enter the real world again. It was time to wipe the slate clean and reinvent myself. I could make it out there in reality. I could participate as a normal human being, right?

It was settled. There was a new Jenny Green in the city, and she'd make her first appearance after some beauty rest, because she was totally exhausted.

Chapter TWENTY-SIX

THE JENNY GREEN
REINVENTION TOUR

Introducing . . .

Jenny Green the waitress!

It was my first day of training at Momma Molson's. My trainer was this cute guy, too.

"Jenny, you're gonna have tons of fun. Let's start with your sidework."

"Sidework?"

"You know, the running sidework you'll be doing while you wait tables."

"You mean I don't just, like, get the customers their drinks and take their orders?"

"The managers said you've worked in a restaurant before."

A girl from class told me to put it on the application. "Right . . . but we didn't have sidework."

"Really? Well, here we do, eh? You're responsible every day to do a hundred roll-ups of silverware."

"A hundred?"

"Yeah, and you'll be refilling ice, wiping down the wrap station, restocking to-go containers, what else, what else. During lunch shifts you gotta take out the trash. Oh, hey, Jacques!"

"I quit."

Introducing . . .

Jenny Green the model UN delegate! Edgar hooked it up.

"Jenny, welcome aboard! My name's Bradford, and I'm the lead representative for our group. We're preparing for the Canadian National Conference in Ottawa. Have you ever been to our nation's capital? Let's see, you're joining up a little late, and the only open spot we have is for the Democratic People's Republic of China. Tell me, how much do you know about the effects of neocommunism in the expanding global market?"

"I quit."

I couldn't believe I didn't think of this earlier. Introducing . . .

Jenny Green the star actress!

Auditions for the spring play *Tommy* were Monday night. What better way to reinvent yourself than by acting?

I entered Molson Theatre and Dave Price, the sort-of-hot stage manager/senior, personally greeted me. "Jenny Green. Looking good. I think we definitely have a spot for you in this play."

This was before I'd even hummed a note. He was totally into me. "That's great news, Dave Price."

"Why don't you go next?"

I took the stage. Now I'd be lying if I said I wasn't a little nervous, but given the past few months, my trepidation hardly registered on the anxiety Richter scale. It was my time to shine:

> *You don't answer my call*
> *With even a nod or a twitch*
> *But you gaze at your own reflection!*
> *You don't seem to see me*
> *But I think you can see yourself.*
> *How can the mirror affect you?*

And that was it. Short and simple. A consoling round of applause from the director and Dave Price in the wings, and then I was ushered offstage.

"What'd you think?" I asked Dave.

"Spectacular, Jenny. Mind blowing! Rehearsals start Monday, and they go Monday, Thursday, Sunday through Christmas. Then we take a short break and pick them back up on the fifth of January. Expect rehearsals to run anywhere from two to three hours. They'll be at night, so it won't conflict with any classes."

"So two to three hours, three days a week. Okay . . ."

"Wonderful!"

I should have been genuinely excited, but in my mind I'd already quit. Too much work to be like what, a giant pinball or something? I mean, I knew I wouldn't be cast as the mother. I resolved to just not show up for rehearsal.

But as I was leaving the theater, a new figure appeared onstage.

"There he is. Our man!" the director said with peculiar enthusiasm. "You're auditioning for the role of Tommy, right?"

"Right." It was just one word, yet somehow it froze me in my tracks. That voice. That voice called to me. So I turned to face the most wonderful specimen on God's green earth. "Hi, Raymond."

"Hello, David. Can you state your name and year, for the record?"

"The name's David Prince. I'm a senior."

At first I thought he said Dave Price, and I squinted to make sure I hadn't gone insane. Then the director repeated the name: "David Prince. It's a pleasure to have you back with us this year."

My prince. My Prince Charming was literally just yards away. He had brown hair, slightly ruffled, and big brown eyes that beamed across the room. He was tan and handsome. He wore a white long-sleeved cotton T-shirt that fit him snugly in all the right places.

He began his audition:

See me, feel me,
Touch me, heal me.

See me, feel me . . .
Touch me, heal me.

Ummm, yeah. I could do that.
Maybe I'd stick this play thing out after all.

Chapter TWENTY-SEVEN

A SERIES OF MISFIRES
LEADS TO A DIRECT HIT

I couldn't believe I was actually going through with the play. I mean, here I was with this messed-up, totally DL past, yet somehow I was expected to interact with all these normal people. Twisted wasn't even the word.

We had a preliminary meeting at Molson Theatre the following afternoon. It wasn't a rehearsal, really, more like an opportunity for everyone to meet everyone else.

Unfortunately, most of the guys were either gay or nerdy or just not altogether cute or interesting. That meant Dave Price and David Prince were literally the only game in the whole production.

Looking around, I could tell the other girls felt the same way. They listened eagerly whenever Dave or David spoke, seized any chance to help with the production, and congregated in every wing where Dave or David might be located.

I kept my distance, unsure of myself, as David Prince became more and more a presence in my mind. It was weird, because he didn't seem like any other type I'd dated. He was simple, fun loving, cultured, helpful, and totally cool. Was I, like, maturing or something?

He asked the group, "Now who knows the answer to this question, eh? What is cooler than a Molson production of a play? Anyone? Anyone? All right, I'll tell you. A Molson production of a play by Peter fucking Townsend!"

We all laughed at that. I think one of the girls drooled. Oh, and did I mention David Prince was Jewish?

Enter Raymond, the director. Like a character from a bad movie, he wore a beret and striped shirt, and he even brought one of those funnel-shaped speaker things to address the actors. "Okay, actors, welcome to *Tommy*! Congratulations on being accepted into the play!"

Oh, big deal, I think basically everyone who auditioned made it into the play. I was cast as Young Lad Number 3, by the way. It's not exactly a career-starting role, but I did sing the opening lines of "Pinball Wizard." Not bad, eh? Other than that, it was a lot of backup singing and dancing, but I was happy to oblige, since it was my first acting gig in boarding school.

Suddenly I was jolted as someone totally poked my love handles. I swatted the hands away. "Just me, baby." Dave Price. Dammit. Wrong one. "Hey, what time should I pick you up tomorrow night?"

"I didn't know we had a date."

"How's eight sound?"

"Eight sounds . . . fine."

"So where do you live?"

Reluctantly I told him. You should've seen the look on his face when I said the freshman dorms: pure sympathy.

Anyway, I didn't really know why I agreed to this date, because it only seemed to confuse matters, but whatever. Maybe outside of this whole play thing Dave Price would sweep me off my feet.

Meanwhile I watched David Prince going over lines with some of the girls. He seemed so helpful; it had to be an act. I mean, come on, who has the patience for *everybody*? Who did he think he was? It was driving me crazy!

When I got home later, my cell phone was ringing on the nightstand. I didn't recognize the number. Don't ask me why, but for some reason I thought it might be David Prince, so I rushed to answer it. "Hello?"

"Hey, it's Sophie. I miss you already. I want to touch you."

Ewww, I thought. Either it was a wrong number or a prank. For kicks I went with it. "Oh yeah?"

"I've been thinking about you all day."

"Well, I haven't been thinking about you. Gross." I hung up.

Then I found my cell phone in my purse. Oops. I'd accidentally answered Chloe's cell! She'd left it in my room last night.

Damn our stupid matching cell phones! But why would someone named Sophie call talking sex?

Because Chloe was a lesbian! I quickly called back and got some retail store, where the clerk told me Sophie had just left. So I scrolled through Chloe's contact list . . . no Sophie.

Great, that was totally my bad. I ran to Chloe's room, but she wasn't there. So I tried calling her cell and soon realized why that wouldn't work. Honestly, where was my brain? Well, she wasn't gonna be happy about this.

I wanted to go to the gym and decided to leave a note under Chloe's door. I wrote the following: *Chloe, a girl named Sophie called thinking I was you. She said she missed your touch and I forgot you were gay so I kind of hung up on her. I am* sooo *sorry!!!*

Chloe was in her room when I came back that night. She shot me an angry glare that quickly morphed into an apologetic one. Still frowning, she ran over to me and gave me a big hug. "Jenny, I'm so sorry. I did something mean."

"Chloe, what'd you do?"

"Well, you know how you told Sophie off and then hung up on her, then left that note? Well, Sophie was one of two girls I was seeing. Cynthia was the other one. And earlier tonight Cynthia was here, and she saw that note you left and got really mad. You got me in trouble with both of them, Jenny!"

"I'm sorry, Chlo."

"But listen. I was really, really mad at you. I wasn't even gonna talk to you. It's stupid, I know. It wasn't your fault. But that guy Dave Price showed up at your door like half an hour ago, I guess as like a surprise, and I kind of told him you were off on a date with someone special."

"Are you serious? I have a date with Dave Price tomorrow."

"I'm really sorry, but I was like really, really, really mad, Jenny! I mean, I totally liked Cynthia and I don't think we have a chance anymore! But I feel bad now, and I'll call Dave if you want. Tell me you're not mad at me."

"I'm not mad at you."

"You swear?"

"I swear, Chloe. But I have to call Dave back. Then we'll get some soy chai lattes and watch a movie. Girls' night."

"That sounds awesome."

"C'est cool. All right, I'll be right back."

I went into my room. There really wasn't a need to call Dave Price, since I could see whoever I wanted, but I guess the situation did need clearing up. I didn't have Dave Price's number offhand, so I checked the phone list for the play. I dialed and waited. . . .

"Yello." I could already tell there was something different in his voice.

"Hi, Dave?"

"Yes?"

"It's Jenny."

"Oh. Hi, Jenny."

"Listen, I'm totally sorry about what happened. I'm not seeing anyone else."

"You're not? What about Dave Price?" Holy F. I'd totally called the wrong Dave!

"Wait. Is this . . . David Prince?"

"It is."

"Ohmigod, I'm so sorry."

"It's no problem. You meant to call Dave Price?"

"Yeah, but . . . well, he stopped by and my friend told him I was off on a date. It was like a joke but, you know . . ."

"You like him? Dave Price?"

"Ummm . . . well. No, not really."

"I wanted to come introduce myself today, but you know, I didn't want to intrude."

"Oh, come on, what a joke. Because Dave Price was like fondling me? Did you notice me grabbing *him* by the waist or squeezing *his* leg?"

There was a brief silence. Finally he said, "Next time we have rehearsal I'll definitely say hi."

"Next time we have rehearsal?"

"I don't know. What are you doing right now?"

"Nothing." I thought of Chloe and girls' night. She'd understand.

"You know about Ditch Molson?" he asked.

"Of course."

"Well, I go to this cool little bar on De Maisonneuve. They don't ID."

"Okay." *Damaisonwhat?*

"I'll come by to get you."

Notify the prime minister. Declare a national holiday. I was going on a date with David Prince!

Now, what to wear?

Chapter TWENTY-EIGHT

CONCRETE'S IN THE DIRT, BUT LOVE IS IN THE AIR

I didn't want Ben keeping tabs on me, which meant sneaking out. It didn't prove too difficult. If Ben did a random bed-check, I had Chloe agree to race into my room, throw on a hoodie, and pretend to be sleeping. She'd then race back through the bathroom and do the same thing in her bed. Easy!

David Prince met me out front. The way the streetlight played off his face made him seem too hot to be true. It filled me with this strange warmth I can barely describe. Under the cover of night we made our way to Ditch Molson.

"Oh my God," was all I could say upon reaching the ditch. It was filled with concrete.

"It must be part of the crackdown," David suggested. "They don't want anyone getting off campus without their knowledge. You know, because of the deaths."

Wow, and to think I was responsible. David sighed. "Well, I have a car. I'm eighteen, so I can go for however long, but we have to get you back in time. Gives us two hours. You like to bowl?"

"Hell yes. We used to go all the time." It was true. Believe it or not, Jenny Green was quite the bowler.

"Let's go bowling," he suggested.

With that we were off. Well, not just yet—it took like half an hour to get back and then a few minutes to get David's car going. Good thing I didn't care about a hot set of wheels anymore, because he drove his dad's old, beat-up Mercury. As I shivered in the passenger seat, he explained, "Heater's broken. It does the job, though."

On the way to the bowling alley, we nicknamed his car "the Icebox." To keep me warm, he grabbed my hand and started rubbing it. Then he breathed on it, and the heat spread from my frozen little hand all the way down to my frozen toes. I was totally defrosting and falling for David Prince!

Bowling was killer. I mean, I was a little rusty, and maybe I wasn't "quite the bowler," but it was fun nonetheless.

Here's the highlight: Jenny Green steps onto the wood. She hasn't been having the best game, but her last few frames suggest she's steadily improving. Now she's sizing up the lane. With small, deliberate steps she advances, and her arm swings back. What grace! What form! She releases the ball, and there it goes, soaring down the lane. It's looking bad for those pins and good for Jenny Green. The ball's going, going . . . *steeeee-rike!*

But wait, I'm still getting to the best part:

"Yes!" I yelled triumphantly.

David and I leaped into the air. In one quick motion we high-fived each other, which somehow transitioned into a hug, which somehow melted into a kiss. A long, deep, warm kiss.

We parted lips and stared into each other's eyes, wallowing in our unspoken chemistry. We both grinned, then kissed again. This time it was shorter but equally intense. When we drew back we were holding hands. He sat down in a chair and I eased naturally onto his lap. That's how everything felt: organic. And this was the best part of bowling.

By the way, Officer Perv was nowhere to be seen.

The time flew, and before we knew it our two hours were up. It was back to campus, where we both agreed the night was still young. "What now?" I asked.

"Got any ideas?"

"Actually, I do."

So I brought him to Lover's Lounge. Thank God they hadn't filled this place with concrete too. Alas, it seemed so long ago that Josh Beck had shown me this little retreat under the Social Studies Building, and I'd be lying if his presence didn't lurk about, but David Prince muted it with his enthusiasm. "I've never seen this place, Jenny! This is amazing!"

And then it happened. Our eyes met in like this short gaze where on some molecular level electricity was generated. His brown eyes became magnets, my eyes became receptors or whatever the word is. I'd never experienced anything like it in my life. It must have lasted like three minutes . . . or five seconds, I wasn't really counting.

He finally broke the silence. "I'm gonna admit something to you, Jenny. The guy onstage who's laughing and having a good time isn't who I am when I'm alone. I'm not saying it's a facade—I do love to act, and I love people, but it's like whatever mood I'm in, that's me, eh? Right now I don't even know how to describe this mood. It's like I just looked at you and . . . how do I even say this . . . it's like I'm in a trance. God, why do I feel like I know you already?"

Because you did know me, David, and I knew you. We were meant to be together. Our lips pressed against each other's. It was so natural.

Later David showed me his townhouse, which he shared with two other guys. You had to be eighteen to live there because there was no housemother or -father. In case you couldn't tell, Molson had some killer housing. Oh, by the way, yes, David was eighteen and I was a minor, but come on. Only in lame America would people *really* care about two high schoolers dating.

"Wanna come in?" he asked. Then he teased, "We have heating." But I wasn't saying anything, just looking at him. "Who are you?" he asked.

God, if he only knew. All I said was, "I want to come in."

We crept quietly into the dark townhouse, and before I knew it David's arms were all over me. He kissed me, first on the lips, then the neck, and then anywhere that suited him. I was doused in warm, wet kisses and totally loving it.

Like two animals we made out on the kitchen counter, unable to control ourselves. Everything felt so right. If he'd taken it further, I didn't know whether I would've stopped him.

But he didn't take it further. Tactfully, he put things to a halt, and for a few minutes we just held each other. "I gotta tell ya, Jenny, you're not normally my type."

"Who is?"

"Someone who doesn't spend an hour picking out clothes or doing her hair."

"I don't think that's me anymore. I don't care about those things, really. I think I was just waiting for the right guy and killing time in between."

"And you think I'm him?"

"Do you think you're him?"

"I think I am."

"I think you are too."

"Let's play a game. Outburst, baby!" he chanted.

"Oh yeah!"

"Sweet," he said. "But before we do, I want to establish something. I know this will seem random, but I just want to get it out there. No sex tonight. Whatever happens. No sex. Not yet."

It was like music to my ears. "Deal."

"All right. Let's do this."

So we played a killer game of Outburst, which somehow

turned into strip Outburst, which inevitably turned into a heated make-out session right there in the den. Thankfully, his roommates were both asleep in their rooms by then. I mean, neither of us were completely naked, but we were both pretty close. It was like four in the morning when we finally stopped.

"I guess I should go." I sighed.

"You can stay. We won't have sex."

"We're practically naked already. Let's do something tomorrow."

"Let's," said David Prince.

And we did something the next day, and the day after that, and the day after that, and the day after that. . . .

David Prince grew up in Montreal, but his parents moved to Quebec City two years ago. David Prince wanted to go to McGill University in Montreal and study to become a sports manager. David Prince played ice hockey until last year, when he tore ligaments in his knee. David Prince was a reform Jew who recently found himself more and more engaged in his religion. David Prince played guitar and wrote music. David Prince bit his fingernails when he was nervous, just like me. He was a righty. He was double-jointed. He knew every Dave Matthews song by heart. He hated George Bush but liked America. He liked to lie in bed and hold me for hours (no, we hadn't had sex yet). He liked to sing famous songs about girls and replace their names with mine. And no, I'm not just copying stuff from his MySpace page. He was a prince. He was my prince.

And this was all in the first week. By December 8 I was utterly and totally in love. We were inseparable. No, we still hadn't done it yet. God, stop prying!

We stayed in and cooked at his place that night. Well, he cooked and I watched. I was excited because I was actually gonna eat. I'd totally regained my appetite.

David said spontaneously, "I have a question."

"So ask it."

He drew me near. We kissed. "Jenny, is it too soon to say I love you?"

No, it was definitely not too soon.

Chapter TWENTY-NINE

TOMMY, CAN YOU HEAR ME?

O n my way to rehearsal I totally spotted Officer Perv again. I wanted to ignore him but couldn't. He was taking this too far, and I was convinced he was following me without permission.

That settled it. I found a pay phone and had the operator connect me with the local police.

"Hi, my name's Jenny Green. About two months ago two officers came by my place to ask me about my ex-boyfriend Danny."

"Daniel Davis?"

"Right. And one of the officers was this dorky guy named Jim."

"Sounds like Jim McDougal."

"Okay. Well, pretty much every other day for the past two weeks he's been like following me."

"Really?"

"Yeah, he's here right now, across the street. I'm at Molson Academy, across from Momma Molson's. It's always the same thing. He just sits there, watching me. Am I like a suspect or something?"

The officer cleared his throat. "Can you do me a favor and just stay where you are?"

"But I have rehearsal—"

"It should only be about five minutes, eh. We're just gonna send a cruiser by to check it out. They won't need to talk to you or anything. But please just wait until you see the cruiser, then you can go on your way."

I was already kinda late. But whatever, it was time to end this thing. I agreed and hung up. Then I waited . . . and waited.

Finally the cruiser appeared next to Officer Perv's Pervmobile. Two cops got out, and I took that as my cue to leave.

I was totally late. Dave Price was especially mad. "Jenny, where have you been? We've been trying to do 'Pinball Wizard' for the past fifteen minutes."

"I'm sorry!" The truth was, he probably requested that they do "Pinball Wizard" as soon as he saw I was late.

Remember how Chloe told him I was off with some other guy and then I called back but got David Prince? Yeah, well, I never really called Dave Price back to clear things up. Then I canceled our date because now I *did* actually have another guy, who was also in the play. Dave wasn't thrilled.

"Listen, Jenny. This is unacceptable. We're thinking about making you Young Lad Number Four and making Shelley Number Three." They were conspiring against us. Dave Price was such a jerk! I couldn't believe I almost went out with him!

"I was fifteen minutes late. How about you just cut off one of my hands instead?"

"Seriously, Dave, let's not get carried away." David Prince to the rescue.

"Stay out of this, David."

"It's one rehearsal," David said.

"Raymond and I have been talking about it. We don't know if Jenny's right for the part."

That got David fuming. "Right for the part! What is this? Broadway? It's a high school production of *Tommy*, you dumbass!"

"What'd you call me? You wanna be part of this thing or not, David?"

"Not if it's being run by some jerk, eh? Get a life, Dave, this won't be your big break."

"Fuck you, David!"

"Fuck me? Fuck you, Dave! And fuck this play. I quit!"

"What? Dave! David! No," pleaded Raymond.

"Hey, this guy's been riding my ass for the past week over nothing. I don't want it. I don't need it. I quit."

Well, that was unexpected. David stormed out of the theater. I followed. I guessed I quit too.

I caught up to him down the path to the parking lot.

"David!"

"What?"

"Don't snap at me!"

"Why couldn't you just be on time? You knew Dave Price was already pissed at us."

"Something important came up. I'm sorry! I didn't ask you to quit! Let's go back."

"What's the point?"

"But you love this play."

"Yeah, when it's on my terms. Dave Price sucks all the fun out of it. It's not worth getting into. Listen, I just wanna be alone for a while. I'll call you later. We'll hang out tonight."

"But David—"

"I'll call you!"

And he was off.

I was angry and dejected and depressed and frightened all at once. I felt so cold and lonely on that corner, more than ever before. Was this how it went? Every time he needed to be alone I'd feel like it was the end of the world?

Tears swelled in my eyes. David, come back! We didn't need the play, we just needed each other.

It drove me insane! How could he just leave like that? Didn't he realize how that made me feel?

Just hours ago I'd been happier than I'd ever been in my entire life. Now I was just as sad. I knew what it was to feel spurned.

If he didn't call me that night, I'd totally lose it.

He didn't call.

Instead he showed up at my dorm room. It was a relief, to say the least. From the doorway he sang, "You've got your ball, you've got your chain, tied to me tight, tie me up again."

"That wasn't nice, what you did to me."

"I'm sorry, babe. I was pretty mad. Then later, when I realized how I just left you there, I was scared. Jenny, I think tonight's the night."

I was already leading him into the bedroom.

Chapter THIRTY

LOSING MY VIRGINITY . . . AGAIN

Okay, this totally deserves its own chapter.

David locked my door and I locked the bathroom door, leaving a scrunchie on the knob just in case. He held me before him. "You're radiant," he told me.

Then he kissed me. Like before, his kisses melted my soul. It was so perfectly warm in my room that I felt little beads of sweat on my forehead. It prompted me to take off my shirt. We made out more, and every so often I snuck glances at the frosty windowpane. Outside, the snow fell ceaselessly; it made it seem that much warmer inside.

My room was kind of transformed to me. It was like David and I had our own private, unusually cramped log cabin somewhere far away. The light hum of music from my laptop drowned out the chorus of pubescent freshmen outside the door. Romantic wasn't even the word. It was mystic. It was transcendental.

We were both pretty much naked without even realizing it. That was how our sessions went—the energy consumed us. We were on the brink of sex. And I was ready. I'd been ready since the moment I'd seen him onstage.

David didn't say a word. He took me in his big arms and set me down on the bed. Then he looked at the designer sheets as if figuring something out.

"I won't bleed," I told him.

"You said you were a virgin."

"A virgin with a dildo," I lied. In all honesty, I felt pretty bad not telling him about Josh Beck, although my cherry had been popped long before Josh Beck came along. Eww, that sounded so gross. But now was not the time to dwell on such things.

David found his jeans and pulled out a condom. He took his time putting it on. I watched. Soon he was back on my bed and on top of me. Everything seemed elevated to another level now. This was the real deal. Jenny Green was having her moment.

He took his time at first. Slow. Smooth. Immediately it was pleasurable. I moaned and sighed. I bent to his will but took control, too. Our bodies melded together so perfectly that I found myself moving without having to think about it. So before long I was on top, partially because his movements put me there but mostly because it's where my body decided to go.

The pleasure was immense now—like nothing I'd ever felt

before. My body was a shell of nerves, every inch of flesh a budding flower. Time was immeasurable and a mere joke in the throes of our passion.

David was on top again and going at it harder because that's where the energy took us. My motions met his naturally and gracefully. It was coming. It was coming soon. His breaths were short and my moans loud. He went even faster, and I was on the verge of screaming in ecstasy. This was all I wanted. Nothing else in the world. Only this.

And just when I thought it couldn't get any better, it did. It grew. It climbed. It came. The big O. Yes! Yes! Yes! Aaaaahhhhhhhhh . . .

Now I really melted. I crumbled. I shriveled into a puddle of gel. A gasp moved past my lips. David let out his own loud sigh of release. He went slower. Slower. Then he stopped. We both just lay there for who knows how long.

We were exhausted.

Chapter THIRTY-ONE

WAIT, I'M FORGETTING SOMETHING

Bored and thinking about David, I signed on to MSN to see if he was there. GreenBee16 was unleashed on the World Wide Web:

GreenBee16: Hey there.

DavidPrince3: Hello, baby. How you feeling?

GreenBee16: I miss you.

DavidPrince3: I can't wait to see you again. Gonna sex you up.

GreenBee16: Oh yeah.

KloheeAngel: jenny!

GreenBee16: Chloe! Where are you?

KloheeAngel: next door. omg I met someone! her names juliette. she's hot.

GreenBee16: That's amazing.

KloheeAngel: yea, the only thing is i asked her what she wants to study and she said ESL. i was like, you can't study to be a psychic in high school! LOL!

GreenBee16: It's ESP. Chloe, just come to my room.

DavidPrince3: I can't see you tonight.

GreenBee16: Why not?

DavidPrince: Got a paper. You know, midterms.

GreenBee16: Holy shit. Midterms! I totally forgot.

KloheeAngel: whats ESP?

GreenBee16: Chloe, I forgot about midterms! They're coming up like this week and I haven't even been to class!

KloheeAngel: OMG!!!

GreenBee16: I have to call Edgar.

DavidPrince3: No, you're not cheating, Jenny.

DavidPrince3: That's why your country is so fucked up.

DavidPrince3: Because everyone cheated to get where they are. I'll help you study.

DavidPrince3: Jenny?

GreenBee16: It's impossible, David. My math class
   is in like another language.

MrAlanGreen: Hi, Jenny.

GreenBee16: Al Green!

MrAlanGreen: You know I hate when you call me that.

GreenBee16: Sorry, Daddy.

MrAlanGreen: Did you get your Hanukkah gifts?

GreenBee16: Of course. Thanks, Daddy!

MrAlanGreen: How are your studies coming along?
   Your mother wants to know when you're coming
   home.

KloheeAngel: what are you gonna do?

GreenBee16: Chloe, just come to my room.

KloheeAngel: oh yea. TTYS!

DavidPrince3: I'll be over tonight to help you study.

GreenBee16: But your paper . . .

DavidPrince3: It's okay. First we'll get you on track,
   then I'll get to my paper.

GreenBee16: What, no sex?

MrAlanGreen: Sex? What about sex, Jenny?

GreenBee16: Nothing, Daddy. Chloe just walked in.
   Gotta go. Love ya!

For the first time in my life, I actually planned to get by on studying alone. That meant no secret cheat mission with Edgar, and no flirting with any teachers to help curve my grade. Well, one last visit to Prof Stone's office couldn't hurt.

I went later that day, after David and I agreed to meet at my place that night. With no time to bake, I stopped by the caf and bought a dozen muffins for Stone and a big cookie for David.

It had been too long since I'd seen my favorite teacher, and last time I'd been all weird, but now I could relate to him eye-to-eye. Love did rule the world. And you didn't have to make it up. It existed. It was real and powerful. It was inside me.

Good old Prof Stone. I entered his office, and he was sitting behind his desk in a robe. I saw his trademark jacket and cane on the tiny couch along with his other clothes. "Prof Stone?"

"Jenny Green?"

"What are you doing in that robe?"

"Oh. Well, you know, it's not my real office hours. Which brings me to wonder how you knew I was here."

"Lucky, I guess."

"No, Jenny, it is I who is lucky. Are those . . . muffins?!"

"For my favorite professor."

"Mmm . . . smells like cranberry walnut with a hint of nutmeg."

"Umm . . . yeah, you got it!" Actually, I hadn't checked the box. I guess Prof Stone received a lot of muffins over the years.

"Jenny, but you haven't been to lecture."

"It's been a scary month. Are you gonna drop my grade?"

"Sounds a little drastic, no?"

"Ohmigod, I totally love you." I gave him a big hug where he sat. It kinda grossed me out, though, that I was so close to his underthings.

"So what brings you here?"

"I've been thinking about love. How do you know when you're in love?"

"How do you know? It's easy. Do you think about him all the time, like he's the only thing in existence?"

"Maybe."

"Do you feel aimless when he's not around?"

"Yes."

"When you're together, does nothing else in the world feel more natural? Even when you're in a fight?"

"Oh my God."

"Are you in love?"

I didn't want to ruin it with Prof Stone, because if he thought I wasn't available then it could affect my grade. So instead I answered, "No. It's my roommate, Chloe. She's just been talking nonstop about her new girl . . . boyfriend. And it's hard for me to relate, you know?"

"Jenny, you're a beautiful, smart young girl. Any guy would be lucky to have you." As he said this, Prof Stone rose from his seat and walked over to me. He brushed my cheek with his hand.

Okay, it was a little creepy. "He won't be who you expect, and he can come from anywhere. He could be standing before you and you wouldn't even know it."

He was definitely coming on to me, but there was no way he'd make a move. Sorry, Prof Stone, you're old and I'm taken. The important thing was, he was still wrapped around my finger.

To seal the deal (and okay, tease him a little), I gave him a nice big hug before leaving. Squeezing him in close, I ran my fingers from his shoulders down his back. I wanted him to remember me when it came time to curve my grade. So it was a little unethical, but for the other midterms I promised myself I'd hit the books, just like David wanted.

I left the office. Glancing back, I saw Stone with a muffin in one hand and, well, adjusting his robe with the other. Are you okay, Prof Stone? I've never seen a robe stick out like that before.

Chapter THIRTY-TWO

STUDYING, SPICE NETWORK-STYLE

On the last night of Hanukkah, David Prince showed up around seven with a stack of old papers, tests, and CliffsNotes. For the first time he wore glasses, and it totally made him look smart.

It was kinda funny because in preparation I'd worn glasses too. In fact, I wore the perfect student outfit that night: knee-highs, a skirt, a button-down shirt with a tight sweater-vest over it. I looked like someone from a boarding school with an actual dress code, and I knew it would turn him on.

Time to hit the books! He used memory tricks and pictures, note cards and games. He was a total drill sergeant, but it totally worked.

Then came time for math. Well, don't ask me how, but AP Calc as taught by David Prince suddenly didn't seem so difficult. Okay, it was still really difficult, but when he tested me on everything I got a C! That would average me out to a B, which I was fine with. Believe it or not, I was pretty smart.

Now, on to the good part. David put the books away and took off his glasses. I took off mine. "Okay, well, Jenny, you've impressed me beyond my wildest expectations."

"There was talk of a reward."

"Yes, now don't get the idea I do this with all my students."

"Sure, sure. I bet that's what you told the last girl."

"Will you still respect me as your instructor afterward?"

"Depends on the caliber of my reward."

And as we played teacher and student, we both casually started to undress each other. It was so hot I'm getting horny just thinking about it.

He undid each button one by one. "I must say you responded really well to the lesson tonight. I think you'll do just fine on the exam."

"Go easy. I'm just a young schoolgirl."

"Young and innocent you are. It's time you entered the world of love."

Our shirts were off. He slid his hand up my bare thigh. You know what followed, but I don't want this book to be like some softcore trash novel (it's got enough sex already) so I'll leave it to the imagination. I'll just say there was lots of foreplay, which I really, really liked.

Later that night we cuddled in bed. Now, I hadn't slept with that many guys, so I didn't know a lot about cuddling, but I couldn't fathom that any other man in the world cuddled like David Prince. He rubbed my back, he spooned, he whispered "I love you" into my ear.

And it was authentic. It wasn't some process served merely for the sake of the girl he was bedding. He wanted the lingering sense of closure as much as I did. He hated that the moment would end.

"So, you ready for a surprise?" he murmured.

"I have a surprise too. Can I go first?"

"Okay."

I went over to the closet to fetch his gift. When I slid open the closet door, I couldn't help but grow acutely aware of the shoe box just feet above my head. Inside it was the incriminating dagger that killed Thomas Baker. Why hadn't I moved it yet? I didn't know. Maybe because I wasn't supposed to even know it was there. The other Jenny Green put it there. It was *her* secret.

I retrieved a small gift box and slid the closet door shut.

David sat up like a little kid. "What'd ya get me?"

"It took me forever to think of."

He unwrapped the paper and opened the box. Inside: a gift certificate. It was good for six hours with just David and his friends at Centre Bell, the ice-hockey rink where the Montreal Canadiens play.

David was ecstatic. He jumped on the bed. He hollered like a testosterone-charged hockey fan. He kissed me from my pinky toe all the way up to my lips. "Jenny, I love you so much. No girl has ever gotten me anything like this. I'm so glad you came along. I love you. Did I already say that? Well, I'm saying it again. I love you. It's like I've known you my whole life. Thank you. Thank you, thank you, thank you."

"You're welcome," I said coyly.

"Well, I don't think I can top that, but now it's time for your gift. I don't have it here, so I'll just tell you. Jenny Green, you are invited to join me, David Prince, on a four-day cruise. I wanna take you to a world without snow. We'll leave the 'Icebox' behind, baby, it's time to fly away with me! What do you say?"

"Are you serious! Ohmigod, David! I say yes! I say hell yes!"

We hugged we kissed and cuddled for hours. I was one hell of a happy girl that night. I was going on a cruise in the middle of winter!

And that was that. We studied hard. We played hard. It paid off. I wouldn't get grades back until way later, but I knew it was As and Bs on every midterm. Even math! Okay, I got a little help from Edgar for like two of the problems, but the rest was all me. Okay, five of the problems. Told you I was smart! Boo-ya!

For a girl who'd spent a semester devoted to everything but school, I deserved a pat on the back but got something better—a four-day cruise with the man I loved.

Chapter THIRTY-THREE

POTHOLES

There were just a few minor potholes that week that left me a little less cheery than would be expected. Actually, they were major potholes. And as luck would have it, they all happened on the same day: Tuesday.

Most of the semester was over by now, and all that was left was my paper for Prof Stone's class. But he'd extended the due date until after Christmas because of the whole Thomas Baker fiasco. If only my class knew how much they owed me.

So I'd just finished my last midterm and David was waiting for me in front of my building. We were gonna take a drive around the city and come back to eat dinner at his place. Oh, and our four-day cruise was in just four days!

A quick peck on the lips. So natural.

"I have one last reward for you," he said. "Hop in."

"Where are we going?"

"Ice-skating at Beaver Lake. It's all the way up Mount Royal. It's frozen over by now. Beautiful, like you."

Just the thought of it made me all tingly inside. Sure, I wasn't the greatest skater, but just the idea of it turned me on. So we hopped into the car, and on the way David ran over this huge pothole. *Thump!* The car lurched, and David instinctively put his arm across my stomach.

"That couldn't have been good for this lump of junk. Are you okay?" he asked.

"I'm fine," I assured him.

Then I looked in the side-view mirror and I wasn't fine: A brown Lincoln was driving recklessly three cars behind us. Officer Perv was totally on our tail! At first glance I thought it couldn't be. He was clearly violating protocol or whatever. But no, it was him, and he was totally pissed off. I was done for.

I started chewing the crap out of my nails. Everything seemed compromised. Soon there came a voice over a speaker: "This is the police. Pull over!"

David was purely confused. "What the hell . . ."

"Don't do it, David. What kind of cop does that?"

But Officer Perv had anticipated our reaction. "David Prince and Jenny Green. Pull over now! I'm not kidding aboot this!"

"He knows our names," David said.

"It's a scam."

"In broad daylight?"

David, not knowing what else to do, pulled over to the curb

in front of a *dépanneur*. I slumped into my seat as my doom advanced in the form of a wannabe cop.

He was out of uniform, which led me to believe he'd been suspended, maybe. It helped ease the tension. Officer Perv shouted, "Hey ya, murderer! Hey, Dave, you know you're dating a murderer!"

"Who the fuck are you?" David yelled, getting out of the car.

I followed. "He's a cop." The jig was up.

Officer Perv was quickly in our faces. With every word came a steamy gust of liquored breath. "You think you've got anyone fooled? You weren't at the library that day. I checked the cameras. You left earlier than you said, eh? Well?"

But I wasn't stupid. Obviously I'd checked with like a hundred employees to make sure that the library didn't have cameras. They didn't. "I don't know what you're talking about, you drunk!" I said. I just couldn't contain my anger.

It didn't matter. Officer Perv wasn't even acknowledging my defense. "Your boyfriend here know how unfortunate you were this year? Does he know about Dan Davis, aka Dizzy D?"

David looked at me. "You knew Dizzy D?"

"Everyone knew Dizzy D, David."

"But not everyone got down on their knees for him, eh?" Ewww, it sounded really weird coming from such a perv. "There's a video, ya know."

Now David seemed a little angry. "You were dating Dizzy D? Was it when he died?"

Officer Perv answered for me, "Pretty much. In fact, she killed him."

David stepped in. "Hey, man, I don't think cops can be drinking on the job. I think I might make a call."

The Perv continued, "She was dating Joshua Beck, too, eh? He supposedly jumped to his death, although they never found much blood. The little they did find was suspicious, to say the least. Then you have Buddy Levine. Killed by a 'freak' icicle avalanche, eh? But we got ourselves a witness, Jenny Green. Says you're the 'freak.' How aboot that? He saw you up there. He saw ya kill Buddy. We already know you were at that party. We already know. Clock's winding down, Jenny. Ya went overboard with Thomas Baker, ya know. The kid was in your class. Ya think that would slip by us? Your number's up. It's just a matter of days now."

David was stunned. The evidence seemed pretty overwhelming when put into perspective like that. It made me wonder why I hadn't been arrested already. No real proof, I guess. But it was probably the library/cafeteria alibi. Thank God for that nerdy librarian and my swipe card.

David wasn't saying anything, and it totally scared me to death. Did he believe them? I hated Officer Perv so much! I mean, look at him with that smug grin. I wanted to rip his mouth off and jam his face into the snow. Then maybe David could run him over with his car. The old Jenny Green would've killed him that night.

I took deep breaths and made myself cry. It was another Oscar-winning performance. I mean really, who would ever believe the sweet girl standing on the curb had ever killed someone?

I replied through my tears, "The police will be hearing about this. They'll be hearing about this right now. Maybe they'll catch you in time. What are Canada's laws on drunk driving, anyway? I think I'll ask Officer Prick, I mean that other cop who was with you at my house."

For some reason this totally worked. It jolted Officer Perv back to reality. He seemed startled enough to sober up. Waving a shaky finger at me, he backpedaled toward the Pervmobile. "Soon, Jenny Green. Soon they'll be coming for ya. Don't think you've gotten away with anything. Not for a second."

I really needed to get rid of that dagger. Officer Perv drove off, and I started bawling.

David just stood there. I could tell he wanted to hug me, but he wasn't sure who it was he'd be hugging.

"It's not fair!" I cried. "Why won't he leave me alone? The deaths were hard enough to begin with!"

"Jenny. Were you at that party?"

"Yes. And I dated Josh Beck and Dizzy D, and Thomas Baker was in my math class. I don't know what to tell you about it. I don't think someone's following me and killing off people. It's been a hard semester, okay?"

"Why haven't you mentioned any of this?"

"I don't know. We were having so much fun. I don't wanna be, you know, like a downer."

"A downer? A downer! You know what's a downer? The cuts."

"What cuts?"

"The cuts. The fucking cuts!" He rolled up my sleeve. "This isn't normal! And now you've been acquainted with four people who died. That's news, Jenny!"

"Two people. I didn't know those last two guys. I just happened to be connected with their whereabouts. I showed up at that party 'cause some guy invited my friends. It's not fair! I didn't kill anyone, David. I mean, come on. He has to be lying about the library. I was there all day when Dizzy died. He knows I was. I don't know why he keeps following me."

"If he was following you, why didn't you tell me?"

"Because I called the police and they supposedly took care of it. That's what we need to do right now. Call the police."

"Okay."

So we did. Then we got back into the car and David didn't say much. He turned to me. "Hey, if you don't mind, I'm gonna head back to Molson. I just need some time to think about stuff."

I almost vomited right there in his car.

I didn't hear from David for the next two days. I'd call and he'd send me to voice mail, then never call back. I'd sign on to MSN and he'd sign off. I wanted to wait outside his house but worried he'd think I was like stalking him.

In a desperate attempt to find out what was going on, I realized I needed to break into his e-mail from my computer. I'd already spied out part of the password when I was at his place the week before and just needed like three more letters or numbers. I knew exactly where to go with my dilemma.

"You want me to what?" Edgar exclaimed.

"I have like six letters, I just need the others. Don't you have some sort of program that can hack me in?"

"Greenie, you never cease to amaze me. In the face of such a drastic few months, you seem totally unfazed."

Yeah, well, I *was* the reason for those drastic few months. "So can you do it?"

"What have you done for *me* lately?"

Jeez, I don't know, saved your life. He was on Thomas Baker's list, after all. Instead I just reminded him of his hot night with Julie, and it was more than enough. He'd only been joking in the first place. I loved Edgar.

So we plugged the letters I had into his program, and after like five minutes the obvious password was staring us in the face: JimiThing. It was a Dave Matthews song, FYI.

I kissed Edgar on the cheek and headed home, where I logged into MSN as DavidPrince3. Going straight to the "Sent Mail" folder, I found an e-mail to one RHatcher234. His last girlfriend was Robin Hatcher. All I knew about her was that she wasn't Jewish, and she was a senior. The e-mail was dated yesterday. I double clicked. Here's all it said: *I keep thinking about last night. It was unexpected, but it felt so good to be back under the sheets with you, Robin. We never should have split up. I never should have seen that other girl. I love you so much.*

He was back with some floozy named Robin Hatcher? I was just "that other girl." That's all I was to him?

Robin Hatcher. The name made me think of some nerdy journalist. And our own Robin Hatcher's got the scoop! She was the third pothole, by the way. *David, do you really love her?* I wanted to ask. I needed to ask. Were we really through?

It was bitterly cold in my room, and I was really scared for some reason. He couldn't be leaving me. He loved me, not her. I knew he loved me. And I loved him. And as far as I knew we still had a cruise together, after which he'd never think about her again.

Chapter THIRTY-FOUR

A DISASTER WORSE THAN THE *TITANIC*

While this is probably the most important chapter, it's too painful to describe in detail. Here's the abridged version of what happened on the cruise: nothing.

It was the day before we were supposed to go, and I was packing. Yes, I know it was delusional, since I hadn't heard from David since our car ride together, but what can I say? I was praying he'd come around.

Then I got the e-mail. Here was the gist of it: *Jenny, I don't think it's working out. I'm sorry. The cruise is canceled. I don't think we should see each other anymore.*

He didn't even have the decency to call. Maybe he was scared. It didn't matter. I was furious. Officer Perv had just given David the incentive he needed to get rid of me and return to her. I was just some rebound in the first place, and David was going back to his precious slam dunk. He was probably taking her on the cruise. I was just some hunk of meat to him.

God, he'd said he loved me. Those words were so euphoric when he'd said them, and now they tore me up inside. It wasn't fair!

There was no David Prince Charming. There was just him and every other guy on the stupid planet, and they might as well all be the same person.

He went on the cruise with Robin the next day. They could sink for all I cared.

·

Chapter THIRTY-FIVE

CAN DAVID STILL GO TO HELL
EVEN IF JEWS DON'T BELIEVE IN IT?

My heart was crushed, yet that wasn't the worst of it. The further away the moment drifted, the more pain would seep into my hollow bones. There was no anxiety, no fingernail biting, just pain. Tremendous, crushing defeat.

I passed the hours in a waking coma. Chloe comforted me with hugs and TCBY, but they did little to mitigate the ache I had inside. We spent some time "enjoying the winter" outdoors. Chloe made snow angels in the pristine white powder; I made snow devils in the sludge. For everything that happened this year, I'd never felt so used.

On the night of December 21, I was sitting alone in the dorm. Chloe was out to a party at Juliette's. David and Robin would be home by now.

Then out of like nowhere, Chloe entered my room, shivering;

or maybe shuddering was the better word. Something was wrong. She walked into my arms and cried on my shoulder.

She was so choked up she could hardly breathe. And the more upset she grew, the more volatile I became. There was a force slowly resurrecting from within. It was a deadly force that didn't tolerate abuse. It sometimes went by the name Supergirl. "Chloe, what happened?"

She spurted, "I . . . was at Juliette's . . . and I was supposed to make Jell-O shots, you know? But I didn't time it right or mix it right and they weren't solid, so . . . so . . . Juliette was drunk and she got really mad and we were outside smoking and she . . . she . . . she dumped the entire ice cube Jell-O shot thing on top of me in front of everyone! Jenny, it was so humiliating. I was freezing cold!"

Poor Chloe. Poor, poor Chloe. My weariness dissolved. I became a statue of myself, made of stone. I petted Chloe until she was calm. After she turned in, I remained in the same position until two in the morning.

I let the old blood rush back into my veins—loveless, heartless blood. I let it drown me in a pool of rage as the old flesh crawled back beneath my skin.

My thirst for vengeance was blind. I wanted to destroy the world. I'd start with Robin Hatcher. Who was I kidding? I'd been plotting my revenge for days and already knew where she lived, just like I knew she was on campus and not home for Christmas break yet.

I was on the move. First I went to my closet, where I fetched a recently purchased pair of cheap gloves, shoes, and a hat. I even threw on sunglasses and another ratty coat I'd never worn. Then I grabbed the shoe box and withdrew the dagger, still inside the plastic bag. Finally it was out the door and to Fairweather Estates, the gigantic house where Robin stayed.

The back door was locked, so I climbed to the second story and found an open window. It led me into the hallway, where I took off my shoes. The house was quiet as a tomb.

Robin's room was 4C—that's what the envelope I stole from their mailbox said. I advanced up another two floors, pausing as someone walked to the bathroom, and found that exact room. Not caring whether anyone in the room awoke, I creaked the door open and snuck in. Both she and her roommate were fast asleep.

Meticulously, I removed the dagger from the bag, then kneeled down beside Robin. The tiny swastika glared in the moonlight. I opened her hand and put the handle of the dagger on her palm. Carefully I wrapped her fingers around the handle and then took the dagger back. Then I hid it in the back of her dresser, where the police were sure to find it (although knowing the local cops, I wasn't so sure).

Quietly I went to her computer and took it off screen saver. Lo and behold, she was already logged into MSN. Perfect.

Now, Robin was born and raised French Canadian, so I had to muster up all the French I'd learned and put it to the test. The e-mail said the following: *Un gâteau est mort. Son nom était*

Thomas Baker. Je l'ai tué. J'regret!!!!!! Je ne sais pas si je peut vivre avec moi-même . . . Au secours! Appelez la police!

The hopeful translation was: *A boy is dead. His name was Thomas Baker. I killed him. I'm sorry!!!!!! I don't know if I can live with myself. Help me! Call the police!* I sent it to everyone on her contact list.

Leaving Fairweather Estates, I knew I wasn't finished. David lived less than a mile away. It wasn't fair what he'd done. It was downright evil. He'd made a fool of me. He'd squeezed all the love from my heart only to let it waste like sour milk.

I marched to his townhouse. It took twenty minutes in the merciless snow. Tears froze halfway down my cheeks. All the way I let the anger build. I wasn't some doll to be bought and discarded. It was evil what he'd done, and now he'd totally pay for it. I'd show them who had the power. I'd show them all: Canadians, Arabs, drug dealers, heart-stomping fake songwriters.

Soon I was there. I had no weapon but my bare hands, but he'd surely have a knife in the kitchen. *David, your number's up,* I thought. *I hope you found the security you needed to die without fear.*

I approached cautiously. His back door was probably unlocked. Stupid trusting Canadians.

It wasn't until I was on the porch steps that I noticed my hand was shaking. It grasped the doorknob but didn't move. What was I doing? Was I really here to kill David Prince? For what? Dumping me? Was that a crime worthy of death? It wasn't. It wasn't at all. God I missed him so much!

I thought I'd put my terrible past behind me. I'd just been deluding myself. I hadn't changed. Then what was I before? I was a monster, that's what. I was a monster who needed to be stopped. Standing at the foot of the door, I realized this had already gone too far. Slowly, reluctantly maybe, I turned around. It was time to walk away. David, why did you leave me?

The snow fell on the quiet, ignorant houses and the ignorant students who lived therein. Outside Fairweather Estates, the wind and snow swallowed my tracks, but this time it didn't matter. Robin would learn a brief lesson, then I'd confess to the crime. I'd confess to everything. I wasn't anywhere near the justice-wielding killer I'd set out to be. I wasn't even sure if I'd set out to be that person in the first place.

I was no one.

Chapter THIRTY-SIX

MOLSON DITCHED

My quivering hand gripped the cell phone. The number for the police was already on the little screen. But I couldn't do it. I couldn't bring myself to press send. I couldn't confess. What would my family think?

I was suffering major guilt, though, in every form possible. Guilt about who I was. Guilt about the people I'd killed or harmed. It was so bad I was totally breaking out, and I *never* break out; well, maybe a pimple here and there, but nothing like the barrage of acne littering my face.

December 22. A Saturday. I was in the nearly vacant freshman dorms. Outside it still snowed, and Christmas was everywhere. On the news, Robin was put in handcuffs and escorted into a police cruiser. It was real. It was international news. It happened. Ironically, there were a lot of people offering her support. She *did* stop a school shooter, after all.

Chloe was supposed to be home with her family already, but when I told her I was staying for a few more days, she volunteered to postpone her departure. As for me, I had Prof Stone's paper and then I'd catch a flight home on the twenty-eighth.

As I sat down to begin, my phone rang. It was a 416 number I didn't recognize. Curious, I answered it. "Hello?"

"Greenie!"

"Edgar . . ."

"Just calling you from home in Toronto. I wanted to wish you happy holidays. I miss you."

"I miss you, too. . . ."

"What's wrong?"

"Everything."

"I get it," he said. "You must be one of those people who get depressed during the holidays. Well, guess what, I'll be back soon enough, and you won't have anything to be sad about."

"You promise?" He did.

It was jarring to hear his voice. It came from a world I no longer knew. You'll be back, Edgar, I wanted to say, but I won't be. I'll miss you. We hung up.

There came a knock at the door.

Chloe didn't move. She just kind of glared at the door in confusion. I rushed to answer it, peeping first through the peephole.

I experienced what you might call relief. Two policemen (not Officers Prick and Perv, thank God) stood in the hall. It was over.

It was finally over. I swung open the door to greet them. "Yes, officers?"

"Jenny Green?"

"That's me."

"We have a warrant to search the room."

"Okay," I said. And I stuck out my hands for them to cuff me. Then it dawned on me that they said the warrant was to search the room and not for my arrest. I brought down my hands and experienced a different kind of relief. I wasn't caught after all. It was totally conflicting, I know.

Chloe rose to her feet. "What's going on?"

"They want to search the dorm."

"What for?"

"Suspicion of homicide," the cop said bluntly.

"Who?"

"Jenny Green."

It was pretty weird, the look Chloe gave me. It was partially one of bewilderment, but also one of accusation. There was extreme anger behind it, as if she were connecting pieces to a puzzle she'd never known was there.

We let the police do their thing. The room was pretty small, so it didn't take long. Chloe said nothing the whole time. They wanted to search her room too. After they finished, she ran in and slammed the door shut.

Meanwhile the cops found nothing (you got nothing on me, coppers, nothing!). They weren't finished, though. The shorter one turned to me. "Jenny, did you go out last night?"

"No."

"You sure?"

"Yes."

Now the taller one spoke. "We'd like you to come down for a lineup."

"What is going on here?" Okay, I started playing the innocent card. It was instinct.

"We can't tell you much. Do you agree to come?" asked Tallboy.

"Do I have a choice?"

"No. Not really. Unless you want to get arrested, let's go."

But we didn't just go. The taller cop proceeded to knock on Chloe's door. Finally she answered. "What?"

"We need you to come too," he said.

Chloe?

They put Chloe and me in the same lineup. Otherwise there were girls who looked totally different from us. It was kind of unfair.

"Number three, will you please step forward?" That was me. "Turn to the right. Turn to the left." Then they had me put on a blue coat, sunglasses, a hat, gloves, etc. Obviously someone had seen me last night, except my coat hadn't been blue, so it must have been from a distance.

I stepped back. Chloe was the last one, number six. She did the same thing. They had her put on a hat and sunglasses and do the whole bit. Total pain in the A.

Finally a somewhat defeated voice came over the speaker. "Okay, number six, please stay where you are. Everyone else is free to go."

I couldn't believe my ears. They wanted *Chloe* to stay? It was a nightmare. Maybe they wanted to interrogate her about me. That must have been it. They were closing in on me. Good. I was too weak to confess, but if they caught me, it was fair game.

I'm sorry, Mom, I thought. *I'm sorry, Daddy. Somewhere along the way things got really, really screwed up.*

Chloe didn't come home until seven that night.

I was wrapped in a ball on my bed, cradling Herman in my legs. I heard her door shut and ran over to greet her. She avoided me.

"Chloe," I pleaded, "what's wrong?"

Her puffy eyes were stained with red veins, her lips were chapped and pale, her face was colorless. I'd never seen her like this, yet she was still so beautiful. "It was you," was all she said.

"What, Chloe? What'd they say?"

"They thought I framed Robin. They thought I killed Thomas Baker. They drilled me for like an hour! You know how I can get under pressure, Jenny!"

"Don't be silly, Chlo. Of course it wasn't you."

"Of course it wasn't me, Jenny. It was you."

"Chloe, what did they put in your head?"

"The cake is dead, Jenny?"

"What?"

"*Gâteau* means cake. The letter you wrote said 'the cake is dead,' Jenny!"

Oops. I meant to put *garçon*. Of all the words to get wrong! "Chloe, I—"

"Here's the thing, though. They found Robin's fingerprints on the dagger, and she doesn't have a solid alibi. For the time being she's still their prime suspect. I don't know. Maybe they just told me that to feel guilty. They said it's why they let me go. But Jenny, if that innocent girl goes to prison or even court, I'll . . ." As she spoke the rage left her and a new expression took its place—pure fear. Chloe suddenly realized she was within arm's length of a cold-blooded killer. She nervously reached for her suitcase.

"Chloe! I don't know what you're talking about. I didn't do anything!"

"They're letting me go home."

"But I need you here!" I cried. I was totally losing it.

"Jenny, we're not friends anymore."

"But why not, Chloe? I didn't do anything!" I was a total wreck. Everything was spinning.

"Maybe you didn't. But there's something wrong with you. I don't know what it is, but please, find a new dorm mate or turn yourself in or . . . whatever. I have a cab waiting."

She was clearly in a rush to get away from me, but I really didn't want her to go. For some reason, losing her was the last straw. She was my salvation. Now she was leaving forever. I'd kill her if she left! No, I didn't just think that.

I begged, "Chloe, please. Take back everything you said. I don't deserve to hear those things! I'm your best friend!"

She didn't respond. Instead she marched out the door and slammed it behind her. I was left alone. No Chloe. No David Prince. Not even Edgar.

I hated the police. I wouldn't give them the satisfaction of my confession. There was only one person I could turn to: Prof Stone. So minutes after Chloe abandoned me, I plopped down in front of my computer and worked on my paper. To warm myself up, I began with my original intent: a paper on the objectification of women in the media.

Soon, however, a new paper took shape, and an essay that started with an analysis of media trends and how they exploit women as objects ended with a two-page confession of everything that had happened. Josh Beck, Dizzy D, Buddy, Thomas Baker, it was all in there.

I even mentioned how Buddy didn't really deserve to die. I'd discovered that he was a big turning point for me. With him I'd gone overboard, and even if killing Thomas Baker was for the greater good, it was too late to take genuine pride in my work.

The final paragraph was a concise, bitter diatribe against myself. I was a shell of the girl I once was. Murder was for savages and idiots. My actions had destroyed me, and all that was left was for someone to come and put me out of my misery.

Here was the ending: *I realize now that no matter how just the killings may have seemed, I was acting on power alone and was thus subject to its laws of corruption. In the end it crushed me. But this is not a plea for forgiveness, rather, it's a plea for execution. If there's a soul, mine is forever tainted, and to kill me is to kill what is already dead, therefore my death shouldn't burden any living person. Amen.*

Okay, the "amen" was a little much, I know. But I suppose in some ways it was a long prayer. A prayer for my death. A prayer for understanding. A prayer for forgiveness (yes, I know I said in the paper it wasn't about forgiveness, but I'm a human being, and forgiveness isn't only for the Christians). I printed the essay.

Without bothering to proofread, I took my confession all the way to Prof Stone's office. On the way I noticed the festive decorations that had been slowly accumulating to the point of totally in your face.

Prof Stone was on his way out, and I bumped into him in the parking lot. "Something's wrong," he noted.

I shoved the paper into his chest. "Read it."

"I have some engagements, Jenny. I plan on reading your papers the day after Christmas."

"Read it now."

"Oh, Jenny, always so eager. For you, anything. I'll be here tomorrow. Five o'clock."

"Good. See ya then. Happy F-ing holidays!"

He got into his car and drove off. I felt no remorse and no regret. I was thrilled. In less than twenty-four hours I'd be found guilty, if only by Prof Stone.

Chapter THIRTY-SEVEN

SO BOARDING SCHOOL WASN'T
REALLY MY THING

I waited like a trained monk. I didn't sleep, not a wink. Nor did I brush my teeth or comb my hair. My features deteriorated. I'm not gonna call myself ugly, but to say the least I wasn't looking my best.

The next day came. Robin was still in jail, although everyone at the station must have known it was me by now. I mean, David Prince must have said something, and I *did* hand a confession to Prof Stone.

Still, the police hadn't come back to the dorm. I couldn't believe it; Prof Stone hadn't called them. Was he that brave? Would he really wait until I showed up to talk to me about it? It was noble of him, and wise; no wonder I'd looked up to him all this time.

Forgetting my coat, I traversed the harsh winds in an old

sweater and jeans. I loved the way the goose bumps covered every inch of my skin.

The faculty building loomed before me. It was my fate awaiting me. Prof Stone would be my judge, maybe my executioner. Well, not my executioner. I mean, he wouldn't kill me, but still, maybe he'd call the police and they'd arrest me and eventually I'd be executed, so in a very roundabout way Prof Stone was like my executioner. Anyway, my life was in his hands, and thus my future would forever be changed just moments from now.

The tension was unbearable. Maybe there'd be cops in the office waiting for me. Some deranged instinct told me to flee the building, then the city, then the entire country, and start anew somewhere random, but I proceeded.

His door was slightly ajar. I knocked.

"Come in," sang the familiar voice. It was friendly, enthusiastic even.

"Hey," I mumbled.

"Jenny, right on time. Gee, looks like someone could use a little rest, eh?"

"You can tell? Sorry."

"No need to apologize. You're still breathtaking. Sit Jenny, sit."

I took a seat across from him. He stood and walked around the desk. Soon he was behind me.

The essay flew from nowhere and landed on the desk. "I suppose you're here for this. Well done." On the first page: A+. It didn't make any sense.

"You deserved it," he said proudly. He scooped up his cane and dallied with it.

"But what about the ending?"

"The beginning, the middle, the ending, Jenny. It was all handled with the skill of a pro. 'The portrayal of women as mere sexual objects is no longer restricted to pornography, but has escalated to a cultural trend.' I believe those were the words."

"Yes, but—"

"Jenny, be happy with your work. You've passed with flying colors, eh!"

It dawned on me then. I would've realized it earlier, but the sleep deprivation had my brain going slow-mo. Prof Stone hadn't read the paper. He'd browsed it, picked up a line or two, then graded it. He didn't take me seriously. He didn't think of me as a "pro." He thought of me as an eager student with nice legs and a big chest.

"Prof Stone, I didn't come here to get my paper."

"I know you didn't, Jenny."

My words were slurred, like some sort of verbal garbage. "No . . . I mean—"

"I know what you mean. And you know what? I came back here just to see you. I could be with my family right now." Prof Stone grabbed my chair and promptly swung it around. Before I knew it I was standing before him. He looked me in my wavering, empty eyes. "Jenny, I can tell when I have a special student. I've been paying close attention to you. I see the yearning in your heart, the yearning for more. You want to live the words of our great poets. You want to know a place where love is king, and I will take you there. I will be your guide."

He dropped his cane and gripped my arms. He drew me near and suddenly we were kissing. His breath tasted like stale cranberry walnut muffins. Gross.

Then we were on the couch, and he was unbuttoning my jeans. I was disgusted with myself, but disgusted with him more. Everything he'd said to me was to get me here. His theatricality in class, his silly outfits, his verbose tangents on love and death; it was all some trick to get to where he was now.

I mean, just five seconds ago he'd paraphrased my paper on the objectification of women, all the while scoping me out like a deer in the crosshairs. I was meat to him and he was a predator, just like the others. He was an unfaithful beast who took advantage of his underage students and didn't do his job. It wasn't much to go on, but I was angrier than I'd ever been before.

It passed like a waking nightmare. First I kneed him in the groin. He let out a grunt, then doubled over and fell to the floor. I found the cane, his trusty partner, next to the couch.

I grabbed his precious gimmick. It was thick but light. A perfect weapon. Raising it high, I cracked him like a hundred times over the skull. *Crack! Crack! Crack! Crack! Crack! Crack! Crack! Crack! Crack!*

I was unchained.

It wasn't just him I was killing. I was killing every man on the planet. Every man who dropped bombs and shot guns and took down beautiful towers. Every man who cheated and lied. Every man who slipped pills. No one was spared. Well, maybe Rabbi Glazer from our synagogue in Long Island was spared, but no one else. I killed both the president and Osama bin Laden. I killed Hitler and Napoleon. I killed Thomas Baker again. I killed David Prince. My hands and the cane were weapons of doom, and they amassed a genocide in a small boarding-school office. *Crack! Crack! Crack! Crack!* Was this enough Eros and Thanatos for you?!

I stopped. Prof Stone was lying on the floor in a pool of you know what.

I couldn't believe what I'd done. It was way too late to turn back. I figured I could get away with it too, but I didn't want to get away with it. If anything, I wanted to get caught as soon as possible. I was lower than them all. I was slime.

Using my Supergirl strength, I scooped Prof Stone off the floor and positioned him in front of the window so that his head leaned against the pane. With a fierce kick I sent him flying through the glass to the snowy ground below.

Away he went for all the world to see. I didn't watch the fall, but I bet he landed directly beside the statue of Molson's first dean.

Soon I could hear a scream from outside. Then another. It was done and I was tired. I was so very tired.

So I sat down on the floor, and waited for the police to arrive.

And waited . . .

And waited . . .

And after more waiting I declared a five-minute rule. . . .

And I ran.

Epilogue

So you're probably thinking this was supposed to be *Jenny Green's Killer Junior* Year, and it was only like four months long, but the title *Jenny Green's Killer Four Months* doesn't sound as good. Besides, when you count all that stuff from sophomore year, it was a full twelve months at least.

Okay, I know I totally flaked on turning myself in, but how much tension can a Jewish girl take? And as I was sitting there waiting for the police (who probably didn't show till like the next day), I decided that prison wasn't a great place for me. So I ran.

It's been a year now. 2007 is over! 2008 is just as messed up! Big F-ing surprise, right? I feel myself changing, though. All the events are becoming vague to me. My wounds are healing. Still, to all those I've hurt: I'm sorry! I truly am! I deal with major guilt over Buddy and Prof Stone every single day. Thomas Baker, not so much.

And readers, beware. The path I tread is lonely. There's not now and will never be a Prince Charming, or a best friend, or a nerdy sidekick for me. They all exist in the normal world with its own rules and regulations, a world I once knew but foolishly chose to leave behind. I'm an abandoned soul drifting beneath the veil of cold night.

I'm in some town that's only a few miles away from the border. I'm going for it and crossing over. F you, Canada!

I miss America. I'm coming home.

About the Authors

At age twenty-four, **AMY BELASEN** has coauthored a novel, is currently working on her second novel and a screenplay with Jacob, and still enjoys nothing more than a frozen yogurt after a long day. After growing up in the New York area with extensive training from the Young Actors Guild and dreaming of starring in her own sitcom, Amy enrolled at McGill University in Montreal, Canada, where a string of breakups practically chased her out of the country. Amy currently lives in Los Angeles and has many more stories to tell.

JACOB OSBORN was raised in Plainsboro, New Jersey, and attended the University of Wisconsin–Madison. While much of the material in this novel stems from Amy Belasen's experiences in Canada, it was Jacob's time in Madison that made Jenny's story of culture shock all too familiar. He now lives in Los Angeles, where he works on both books and screenplays and waits tables. He met Amy while working at a barbecue restaurant and sincerely hopes that, thanks to their partnership, he won't have to spend too much more time waiting tables.

Once upon a time,
I did **not live** in Shady Pines.

Once upon a time,
my name was **not Alice**.

Once upon a time,
I didn't know how lucky **I was**.

LIVING DEAD GIRL, *a novel by Elizabeth Scott*

- -

Need a distraction?

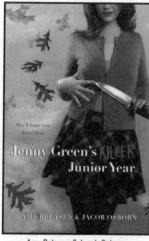

Amy Belasen & Jacob Osborn

Anita Liberty

Julie Linker

Teri Brown

From Simon Pulse

Published by Simon & Schuster